The Swing
and two other stories

This book introduces to English readers an Italian writer of distinction and growing reputation in her own country.

It contains three long stories similar in outlook but strongly contrasted in subject matter and characterization. Their titles are *The Swing*, *The Bridge, and Demetrio*.

Translated from the Italian
by W. J. Strachan

THE SWING
and two other stories

BY

VERA
CACCIATORE

Eyre and Spottiswoode

LONDON · 1959

© *1959 Eyre and Spottiswoode*
Printed in Great Britain by
Butler and Tanner Ltd.,
Frome and London
Catalogue No. 6/4175

Contents

The Swing

I

I HAD THIS STORY from Alessio himself. To steep
myself in the atmosphere of it, I spent an in-
ordinate amount of time on the outskirts of his
native town where I chanced to arrive six months
after the Anglo-American troops had passed through
it. I was present at what they were pleased to call
Alessio's capture, which took place on 30th June last
year, since when I have spent my whole time collecting material about Alessio and Lorenza. At relevant
points in this account I could, if I wished, call upon a
series of eye-witnesses. I could give Alessio's story
according to the parish priest of San Prospero; his land-
lady, Mariannina de Pasquale; Telesforo, the baker of
the shop in the *Piazzale dei Martiri* or finally according to the head of the Asylum ward where Alessio is
at present detained. And as you read my account you
must not forget the background against which Alessio
grew up nor the circumstances of Lorenza's upbring-
ing. Alessio's narrative contains many references to
this setting and I shall therefore make frequent
allusions to it myself. But this is not the moment to
talk of his origins or his early youth. If I thought it
served any useful purpose I would certainly draw on

11

the above-mentioned accounts, but that would mean bringing each of the authors before the curtain, involve a consideration of their characters, backgrounds, and their links with my hero. And this, far from lending clarity to my story, would merely tend to make it a complication of settings, characters, and events of secondary importance and interfere with my narrative.

What I am telling here therefore is the story according to Alessio himself as I heard it from his own lips and as I have pieced it together as best I could. But in addition to Alessio and Lorenza, a third person will also appear and receive full-length treatment. Without this third person – which is in point of fact the place where it all happens – many of the incidents would remain incomprehensible. I am choosing this moment, therefore, for introducing and describing in some detail this strange spot in Central Italy, situated on a hill more than thirty-five miles from the sea, with no railway service and the site of a gradual subsidence of land that has been caused by underground rivers.

According to the geologists the city has been affected by landslides for five centuries and a half. Today, seen from the valley, it looks like some vast, crenellated castle that has somehow contrived to retain its medieval aspect. Enclosed within the curtain walls, access is through four gateways named after the four cardinal points of the compass. Not a single building stands outside the walls. The nearest one to this medieval ward is the church of San Prospero which lies just over a mile away from the *Porta Nord*, and it was precisely twenty yards from the church that the subsidence occurred. On calm days you can see as far as its rim when the gulfs and chasms appear in all their desolation, often completely bare of vegetation owing to the drought, which is the bane of this region, with its many changes of aspect caused by frequent landslides.

At certain times of the year peasants who are bolder and more venturesome than the rest chance sowing a few grains of wheat or oats in the bottom of those gullies where space is not too constricted, and even reap a harvest of a sort. At such times, seen from above, it is as though some blessing from heaven had descended on this desert of red dust. Solid geometric patterns in bright green spring into being, too often destined to disappear beneath an avalanche of crumbled earth which slides silently down; though precisely where these avalanches occur the monotonous outline of these uniformly eroded cliff-walls makes it impossible to establish.

These landslides are like waterfalls that have been rapidly swallowed up in some hemmed-in lake. They plunge heavily on to the motionless surface, to the accompaniment of a vapour-like dust.

You are witnessing the advance of the desert – the earthquake on the march, as the local inhabitants put it. But there is no record of when the earth first began to collapse. Progressive erosion has engulfed the

most ancient Etruscan necropolises, the church of San
Giusto which was re-erected in the seventh century, a
Benedictine monastery and houses of the hamlet which
clung round the skirts of the hospital. The hospital
walls still stand, but the hospital itself was evacuated
about ten years ago. Barbed wire has put a brake on
the curiosity of visitors who at one time used to ven-
ture within the perimeter of the ruin. The crumbling wall shows cracks out of which grow tufts of wild
flowers and fig-plants; capers also strike root there in
the spring, their lilac-coloured flowers blooming in
July only to wither before anyone picks them; and the
lizards bask in the sunshine undisturbed by the
passer-by.

The hospital garden is already disintegrating and
its outside wall is partly sunk in the earth. In the
lower rooms where the waiting-room, kitchen, and
female quarters were situated and where lovers and
sweethearts repaired on holidays to escape from the
midsummer heat and curious eyes, snakes now glide
between the bricks and in the empty window embra-
sures. The carrion crows have turned the second floor
into a parlour, and their discordant cawing never
ceases. They fly to and fro between the hospital and
the campanile, and when they move in the direction
of the city, girating like a merry-go-round between the
Porta Nord and the *Porta Sud*, the inhabitants know
that a storm is blowing up and no one ventures to
mount the cliffs known as *Le Balze*.

Calm, sultry and patient as the periods of good weather are up on those heights, the storms are terrible and of an almost unimaginable violence. The most varied winds seem to collide on the edge of the landslides and hurl themselves against each other with such ferocity that they madden the weather-cock that stands on guard on the campanile desperately trying to decide their direction. And the creaking cry it produces is drowned by the fury of the winds which buffet it as it sends forth its lamentation.

Whirlwinds like water-spouts suddenly surge up from the chasms below, lifting age-old stones and lumps of rock and hurling them on to the fields and roadways where they can be found later strewn for the radius of a mile. It is in fact this kind of after-tow in the wake of the storms that is responsible for the dearth of trees at *Le Balze*.

The inhabitants of the valley hold the souls of the departed in this necropolis to blame for these violent squalls. Country folk will even swear that they have seen a hand groping in the churchyard as if it were striving to snatch some holy talisman to appease some troubled soul. The cross on the top of San Prospero has been wrenched off on several occasions during these storms, and in the parish records its reinstatement appears as a recurring expense.

I cannot imagine how before the period of the landslides the village ever withstood these hurricanes and how a hospital ever came to be built in such an unsuitable locality. The inhabitants of whom I inquired claim that these violent storms did not occur twenty years ago, and attribute the phenomenon to the collapse of the earth which has produced new gullies and chasms, which in their turn cause these eddies and cross-currents of air. It is a fact that in Etruscan times the circumference of the place was five miles greater than its present size and as a result the town trade began to develop where the cliffs now stand, so that it would seem unlikely that the atmospheric disturbances then were as violent as those of the present day.

These unannounced storms occur particularly in the months of November and February. The summer is dry and stable and on some August evenings and moonlit nights the clouds attain a remarkable height.

When I pushed forward as far as San Prospero for the first time, summer had already begun. It was nightfall. *Le Balze* were grey and parched-looking, but down below in the ravines, the earth showed pink, fresh, and humid. A pair of oxen were grazing on the edge of the cliffs, and the sound of the bells fell muffled on the empty air with their vibrations slowed down as if they were under water. Owls of the kind that nest in cliff walls were calling, but it was impossible to determine the precise whereabouts of their cries. The large hospital building stood massive against the pink sky, while the bell of San Prospero calmly rang out the hour behind me.

White linen lay stretched out to dry on some sun-scorched shrubs, surrounded by turf which was so parched that it crumbled at the slightest touch. The washing bellied out like a ship's sails.

Whether it was their resemblance to sails directed by an invisible wind, whether it was the silence of the place in association with the yawning gulf below me I cannot be sure, but I certainly got the impression that the sea might suddenly come up and, by the laws of lunar attraction, fill the space it had previously evacuated. Even the cow-bells with their leisurely ring reminded me of those that fishermen attach to their nets at night when the swell of the waves lifts them and the bells produce a mysterious muffled sound.

The fascination of such a spot for the person who likes solitude is evident enough. The idea that these chasms are imperceptibly advancing increases the spell. And one begins to wonder anxiously where they will come to a final halt and what natural phenomenon or new dyke will ever stop the earth crumbling away in this perpetual erosion.

As one pauses on the rim of *Le Balze* one may be forgiven for harbouring the fear that if this erosion goes on it may well devour whole acres of inhabited or arable land and residential quarters and that no one will be successful in inventing in time any measure to counteract this vast destructive force.

It is on this plateau that the story I propose to tell you takes place. For a period of four years Alessio had

T.S.—B

been in charge of the restoration of San Prospero and for about a year he was also custodian of the church and lived there in solitude. The authorities of the Fine Arts Commission have for some time now been in agreement with those of the church concerning the proper steps for the removal of works of art from San Prospero in view of the land subsidence, and as a matter of fact Alessio had been charged with the task of drawing up an inventory of the contents and of restoring the deteriorated items which might suffer further damage in the process of removal.

It was in this lonely place that Lorenza first encountered him. And it is with him that my story – or, according to Alessio, Siegfried's story – is concerned.

II

It was July when I set out to find Alessio for the first time. He was in garden number 4, the so-called "garden of new-arrivals", reserved as it was for patients still under observation. A vast, rectangular garden surrounded with high brick walls.

Palm-trees and islands of grass constituted the sole vegetation. The planting of other trees was intentionally avoided for fear the patients might break off branches and do themselves or other people injury. But the palm-fronds waved well beyond their reach.

The patients were sauntering along macadamized roads which unrolled like arabesques round the small green islands of grass. Others idled on benches which were lined up under shelters with corrugated-iron roofs. They wore aprons of the kind bakers have, of undyed cloth and without a belt, and they had been issued with a fore-and-aft cap of military pattern as a protection against the sun.

Inside a wooden hut by the entrance, the male nurse on duty was keeping an eye on the patients. He it was who pointed out Alessio to me. He was sitting on the edge of one of the benches. His head, uncovered, had recently been cropped short. His eye-lashes, which were thick and one of his striking features, showed him to be the blond man I had remembered, but he had grown much thinner.

When I took a seat on his bench, a little distance away from him, he raised his eyes and stared at me. They had a greenish glint like still water and played over my face like a searchlight. He was endeavouring to remember who I was, and soon he looked utterly desperate as he lowered, so to speak, nets, hooks, and eel-baskets, everything he'd got, into the depths of his memory to fish out whatever might lay hidden there.

It was at this point that I extended my hand and greeted him by name and title.

"Alessio Marchi, professional restorer," he repeated rapidly, returning my handshake. He trusted that I would forgive him but he had no recollection of me. Perhaps I was one of the people from *Le Balze* or a pilgrim from San Prospero. He had seen thousands of them in his time, he said, visitors or pilgrims, and he would recognize some of them on the site but in this barracks of a place it was not possible. They all felt so worn out by their daily routine and exertions. He could find no time to delve into his memories. In his periods of recreation – as at present – he had to complete his "Plan". He deplored the fact that he did not even possess a fountain-pen and that he had no records at his disposal. Committing everything to memory – and it was always a matter of hard figures – became a slow and exhausting labour. He explained to me that he had divided the country into one thousand three hundred and fifty zones. He proposed to spend six days in each, doing his clearance work. Allowing for time spent in journeys, accidents, and the closing of some of the churches that were being repaired, he reckoned that he had twenty-two years' work ahead of him.

"So you will realize," he said, "that time presses."

He would be twenty-four years old in August, and by the time he was forty-six he would be a free man – and his country too would be free. He hoped by then he would have found collaborators willing to go abroad where the work would be more difficult because of the language problem, the great distances and newness of the ground to be explored. He admitted to me that in the place where they kept him forcibly shut up they considered that he was particularly highly-strung just because one day he had started asking, entreating, and finally crying out to be set at liberty.

"But, as you see, no one listens to me. It is rare for anyone to accord me the attention that you are now giving me."

His friends in the place suffered from a similar restlessness, or so it seemed to him, and they too had plans to work out. The servants and staff were too busy obeying orders; but if only some outsider could start his work for him. He needed a practical assistant so that he could devote himself to completing Plan A. He named it thus to distinguish it from other future plans. Plan B was already drafted; it had reference to the assembling of the works of art removed from the various churches. Numerous museums would arise, and there would be repositories for material that was neither valuable nor artistic.

"If only I could have some assistants," he repeated. But it was not easy to find any because of the risks involved – fury of crowds, arrest, imprisonment, the possibility of being taken on occasion for a thief and a vandal.

While he walked to and fro, talking to himself half aloud, only one solitary voice could be heard in the courtyard. It emanated from a patient leaning against one of the outer walls. A metallic voice, issuing orders to an invisible platoon, monotonous, precise instructions covering every possible drill movement in a shooting range.

"It is no easy job to bring any individual mission to a satisfactory conclusion in these days of such wholesale organization," confessed Alessio. "What with police-stations, telegrams, circulation of descriptions, blockhouses, we are soon identified and watched as 'dangerous'." He had only carried out one mission and here he was in consequence interned and forced to be idle.

I interrupted him at this point to ask how long he had been conscious of his mission and whether his vocation dated far back – from childhood, for example.

"Oh no," he said.

Then suddenly he gripped my arm and stood up. He looked down on me with an expression in which terror was mixed with amazement and disgust. A shudder ran through his lean body under its nondescript apron. The weary look had returned to his green eyes and they roved round interrogatively as much as to say "So you weren't aware of that?"

I too rose to my feet. I felt ill at ease under his stare. I realized now for the first time that my inquisitiveness had brought me into contact with a man whose mind was genuinely sick. Indeed the purpose of my visit had been to ascertain his real condition. There had been so many contradictory reports about him in the town. Some thought of him as a hero, others as a fanatic who should be kept under lock and key and even "exorcized".

I called to him by name, "Alessio," and stretched out my hand. But he merely frowned and shook his head as if he could not really expect this attention even from a friend. And he seemed to be trying to convey that I did not yet know what he wanted to tell me.

And during that pause (it seemed interminable) the bell rang out and a cry of "All indoors!" The voice came through a megaphone which protruded through a barred window.

Alessio shook himself as it reached his ears, pressed my hand and rushed off, whispering, "Go home, Signore. Come back tomorrow and I'll tell you the whole story. I'll tell you about Siegfried – don't forget to remind me."

Slowly we made our way to the gate along with the other visitors. Alessio had begun to speak again and calmly he told me about "Sigfrido", Siegfried, the German hero who by bathing in dragon's blood had learned the language of the birds.

"Here I am, Signore, I too am Siegfried. No, I haven't learned the language of the birds but I know all the rest, now the time has come to tell it to you – I have learned it from the blood of Lorenza."

He had murmured this last phrase hurriedly in my ear and when I was already on my way out of the ward and the gate was creaking behind me and I was complaining that they ought to oil it because it got on people's nerves.

III

I returned to Alessio the following week. Meanwhile the wind had come to the city, a periodic wind peculiar to the place that continues to blow for three days. It can blow up suddenly in any season.

Standing at the Cliffs you can see it as it starts up from thence; it looks like smoke or a spout of steam. It plunges down, bringing with it earth from the ravines. Hard, dry earth of sandy consistency and pink in colour, pervasive and penetrating. In the country it lands under cart-wheels, in the town it finds its way under doors and into crevices; grates on your teeth, is drunk down with water, insinuates itself between your sheets and gets under your eyelids.

It is customary among the inhabitants to shut up their houses and cover up their furniture at the first signs of the wind. But the red dust penetrates everywhere. Some say it has even been known to find its way under the tombstones, and at the canning plant at the *Porta Ovest*, which deals with the export market, it has been necessary to devise a special method of shutting up the premises to keep grains of the dust out of the contents of jars of preserve that have already been prepared for sealing.

This pervasive and irritating dust is extremely noxious to nervous subjects. Two hours of this wind and roofs, streets and gardens are covered with an opaque blanket, and it is a nerve-wracking experience to hear the discordant sounds which accompany it during the three days when it blows.

Inside and round the houses there is a clattering and creaking from a great variety of objects as they crash, sway or fall, and even the buildings themselves shake in the wind's noisy fury. The bells of the twenty-nine churches which the town harbours are swung violently about and begin to ring of their own accord, sending out a truly frenzied peal. Some beat a single stroke and fall silent; others keep on ringing with their silver tongues as if they were attached to the collars of a flock of sheep that never stops moving; others again peal out angrily as if they were trying to break free from the bell-rope, toss to and fro and boom out in loud tones.

At night the lamps in the deserted streets, suspended from the cable in the middle of the roadway, swing like bells, and the beams of light, jerked violently upwards, search out the roof-tops and the constellations of stars in the sky.

As the third day of the gale came to an end I went back to the observation ward and sought out Alessio in the courtyard of the "New Arrivals". I found it empty and the grounds, drives, and corrugated shelter roofs covered with a layer of red dust. The opaque consistency of this fake snow-storm was undisturbed by any footstep, and in the growing shadow the place had the air of being decorated for some ceremony or theatrical performance. Submerged as it were behind these high walls, the courtyard was ominously quiet.

Gusts of wind still pounced on the fans of the palm-trees, shook them, now succeeding in reversing them, now in raising them vertically in the air then thrusting them down again. The huge leaves swayed, cut by the beams of the setting sun, like unsheathed sabres, and stabbed menacingly at the void around them for a radius equal to the length of their own stalks. Agitated by the wind, they were the only things that refused to harbour the ubiquitous red dust.

It was this, which, penetrating into the cracks in the ground-floor windows, was responsible for the crunch of footsteps along the corridors and down the flights of marble steps. The wind whistled along the empty vestibules and in the room on the second floor where the patients had collected together.

I discovered Alessio leaning against the bars of a window which gave on to the piazza opposite the ward. He did not acknowledge my greeting, nor did he turn round when I whispered his name twice in his ear; but his lips moved as if he were talking to himself.

Everybody else in the room was silent. The male nurse in front of the entrance-door was reading his morning newspaper. Two patients, sitting astride a bench, were absorbed in a solitary game of patience which they were playing with a pack of poker cards. Alessio did not even turn round to look at me. Then

I moved up again and whispered the name "Siegfried" in his ear.

Thereupon he swung round and smiled at me.

"Siegfried, at your service. Yes, Signore, so you recognize me then?"

As I was unable to – under that name at any rate – I replied, "Yes, at San Prospero delle Balze." And I went on to say that he had promised to tell me the story of his vocation and the details of "Plan A" with full explanations about the magnificent transformation of Alessio Marchi, the Restorer, into our hero, Siegfried.

"I began after I had made the acquaintance of Lorenza. She came to San Prospero on one of those squally days – in November it was. I wonder, Signore, whether you can conceive of the loneliness of that place in the winter when it pours with rain or the storms are raging."

He expatiated at some length on the loneliness of the spot. I had not at that stage begun to make full notes of what he said, as I was to do subsequently; having to be cautious to avoid arousing his suspicions I contented myself perforce with a fragmentary account.

Yet I have a very clear recollection of the spider episode which he was eager to tell me in order that I might realize the point of exasperation he had arrived at, with so much work to do unaided in the winter. This with the continual presence of a landslide which – as it seemed to him – must advance at night especially during the periods of rain-storms, ready to swallow him up although the commission of inquiry did not in fact anticipate a movement of more than two or three inches a week.

It had been at eleven o'clock at night, he explained. The wind had been blowing for three days and it was half-way through November. While he was undressing he saw a spider dangling down next to the chest-of-drawers. He had noticed it during the past month, and on waking up each morning, had greeted it. It had begun as a kind of joke, but now he wished it good morning in all seriousness. After all, it was a way of communicating aloud with another creature. Indeed, he added, he was fully aware that it merely provided him with a pretext for hearing his own voice and escaping from the incubus of thinking himself mad.

A fat, white diverting spider it was, and it usually confined its activities to the space between the chest-of-drawers and the clothes-stand. Alessio would watch it as it cowered in the corner of its circular web. He blew on it, forcing it to swing to and fro; he tickled it with a blade of straw and laughed as he saw it collecting itself ready to roll into a ball. Sometimes, to his amusement, the spider made a rapid descent to the floor and then climbed back again.

One evening – for the last six days there had been no visitors at *Le Balze* – Alessio had undressed at the usual time and had flung his garments one after the other on to the single arm of the clothes-stand in order

to avoid damaging spider or web. He bid the arachnid
good night. He had certainly never dreamed that it
would be able to reply nor had the idea ever occurred
to him that he might understand its language, if indeed it had one. A spider is a very different proposition
from a hornet or bumble bee that attract your attention with loud and monotonous buzzing. Nor is it like
the moth whose wings beat with unceasing persistence
against the lamp. The summer is a pleasant season,
alive with the hum of insects that are never silent and
always in a hurry. Summer which is led in by patient
columns of ants to contemplate whom is to forget one's
own impatience.

"The summer was still far away in the distance for
it was November when I found my sole companion in
a spider – and a dumb friend at that. No," Alessio
repeated, "although Siegfried was so to speak hidden
inside me at that time, he made no attempt at that
time to learn the language of insects nor even, as yet,
that of birds."

The white owl used to whistle like a train coming
to the points. The little owls screeched from the top of
the hospital wall. The crows played their castanets on
the cupola, campanile and cross. But not on that
particular evening.

The wind was blowing in fitful gusts – with all its
age and weight it thrust against the main gate. Then
suddenly it dropped. In the vacuum that followed – an
ominous pocket of silence – Alessio caught a new sound

– a slow tapping – a regular tap-tap, deliberate, and purposeful. It came from the direction of the chest-of-drawers.

"It's that old scamp again. He's hanging from his thread of saliva, exercising himself behind me, stretching his legs," Alessio thought aloud. "And every time he swings out he is catching against the edge. He'll damage himself if he doesn't watch out."

The creaking and drumming went on however. Alessio commanded silence, but it was no use. The rhythmic tick-tick continued to punctuate the darkness.

Alessio sat up in bed and called out. He shouted the word "spider" several times. He whispered it and then bawled it out so the creature could not help but hear. No reaction. His voice merely reverberated in the void and came back to him exhausted, beat against his ear-drums and roared inside his head.

"Then," said Alessio, "it suddenly occurred to me that he did not stop because I was not calling him by his family name. But he had one, that was certain, and I decided, gale or no gale, to go down to the town next day and procure a book on arachnids so that I might identify this one's name."

This crazy scene had been enacted in the darkness for more than half an hour.

"He's obstinate as well as insolent," said Alessio, "but who knows how scared he is just now as he hears me shout at him. How this poor dumb creature must tremble, knowing me to be so huge compared with him and possessed of such powerful breath. Perhaps his trembling is caused by fears that are beyond his control."

Alessio had lit the light, jumped down from his bed and strode over to the corner. Between the wardrobe and the clothes-stand in the corner the insect was crouching motionless in a corner of its web.

"I looked at his white, swollen circular abdomen. I noticed the point where he was attached to his web and the thread-like claw on each of the eight legs that radiated from his body. Poor creature, poor tiny creature. There he was, half-dead with fright, terrified by my shout. And I called out again close to the drum of his abdomen but endeavouring not to disturb his taut web with my breath. He did not move nor give any indication of having heard my voice. I touched him with my little finger and now, as usual the spider began to travel sideways in a series of expanding and contracting movements. Now, for the first time, I believed that he had not heard me and was continuing not to. Then I began to shout at him, hurling violent, incoherent words and names into the void. But my cries merely came back to me. I insulted him, called him everything I could think of. I kept my eyes fixed on him, imploring him to put an end to his smooth transversal journeys. But he did not hear me.

"He did not hear or did not listen. He was indifferent to my scolding. There I was, as I saw myself in the wash-hand mirror, huge, barefoot, the camel-hair blanket draped round my shoulders. I who was afraid of my own self had given refuge to an unknown species of spider as light as a feather – a spider that lacked a surname – and there I was crying out in the middle of a desert unheeded and unheard."

Alessio informed me that at this juncture, as if he had woken up with a start, he had seized a book and flung it at the spider which, weak and inarticulate, had scurried down in a panic, abandoning its web.

The creaking had started up from the chest again. The darkness which had been mounting now reached its peak, stopped and gave way to a dazzling white dawn. Morning appeared cold and transparent. The wind had dropped.

"It was the morning of my seventh day of solitude and the morning of my meeting with Lorenza."

IV

In the days that followed I never stopped urging Alessio to resume his story. One time I would find him in the courtyard, another in the ward, and I did my best to evoke a response from the instrument that called himself Siegfried. Lorenza was seventeen years old when she arrived at San Prospero on that seventh day, carrying a bundle of laundry under her arm. She was the niece of a farmer's wife who for some months had been washing and starching Alessio's linen for him, and she lived down in the valley, a mile or so away from *Le Balze*. A native of Sardinia, with both her parents dead, Lorenza had been living for the last year with her uncles who were farmers at San Masseio.

As I remember her when Alessio introduced me she was dark and timid; her greenish hair was like floating seaweed, she had regular pointed teeth, was nimble on her feet and never still for a moment. She smiled now and again but she did not seem to know how to laugh. But she could smile beautifully that slow quiet smile of hers.

"How had she learned to smile?" was the question Alessio asked himself, amazed. "Who had she learned it from?"

"Horses," had been Lorenza's reply.

Had Alessio ever seen them when their harness was removed, at night, in the open, their noses pressed against the hurdle, in pairs, close together, with their flanks gleaming with sweat? And their mouths open, revealing their black gums. Their proud eyes that can see in two directions. Look! They hardly raise their lips but their teeth show and it is like an edge of foam when the white waves beat on the shores of Sardinia.

"That's where I had my home, Alessio. My pulse must have beaten four times for every wave that fell in fair weather, and the sea stretches out for miles towards the North and South as it calmly divides. And only beneath the lips of the horses, black as the sea at night did I find the flash and smiling foam that falls

from the lips of the waves. Come, Alessio, come and
see my horses!''

"I fell in love with Lorenza. I covered her with
kisses as she lay on her bed or in the hayloft; even on
the steps into the church nave. Impulsively at every
hour of the day or night; and in the corn too as it grew
tall. She would give me long, faintly distracted glances.
Slowly and in silence she would dress again, slipping
on her red cotton dress which reached just below her
knees. 'Let's get away from here!' she would say if we
were in San Prospero. 'It's a dismal place. I don't know
how you can stand it.'

"She always wanted to run about afterwards,
plunge into the river half-way up her legs, wearing
her wooden sabots that she could never manage to
keep on. It was quite a tricky business, fishing them
out of the stony river-bed, or searching for them
among the poppied corn, or digging them out of a
straw stack in the loft. She used to fasten them to her
belt and go barefoot even over the rough paths, wet
grass, and thick mud. Agile as a lizard, light as a ghost.

"Lorenza mia, my darling one. I can still see you
hanging from the balcony, barefoot, as I saw you then,
rigid, your chin sunk on to your breast in the pensive
attitude which was the prelude to your outbursts of
anger. Your hair hung over your eyes as it always did.
Your eyes were still green. How luxuriant it is, I said
when I first thrust my hand into her hair. It grows
from your head like seaweed. *My* seaweed, I said. She

seemed to take her character from it . . . her free
ways, hopping about continually, always lively. . . . I
am touching you, Lorenza. I used to grasp hold of it.
I was conscious of her swift movements even when she
slept by my side, like a waterfall always ready to
empty itself into the earth, ready to vanish from me.
. . . The thought terrified me. I would cling to her hair
again, loose it seemed, lank and damp like seaweed
piled up to dry along her brown neck where it had not
yet been plaited.

" 'Lorenza!' I am waking her up. It is raining.
'What if it is!' We stayed there lying side by side. It
is April. The rain-drops fall heavily, beating down on
the mulberry leaves.

"That was just like Lorenza. I say 'It's raining' and
she does not move. 'Indeed,' she says, 'why shouldn't
it?' 'But you are getting wet.' 'It's only rain,' she
replies. That's Lorenza. She never retreats. From
whatever side nature approaches, you just watch it.
You mustn't run away. I do not. Nature flows over us
half-naked as we lie merged. Lightly it covers us with
a layer of wetness. It slides down our foreheads,
cheeks, on to our throat and neck. . . . And now I see
it on her neck. Take it away! Take it away for pity's
sake. It is dark, greasy rope, a rope for tying up crates
. . . only a short while ago it was used to tether a cow
near the manger, calm and warm — I can hear the
pails clashing together waiting to receive the milk and
rattling in the cattle-stall like the cymbals of a military

band, intolerable. Quickly, a voice calls out to me, pull
the rope away!

"But it occurred to the militiamen to cut her down
. . . it was just after midday and the wind was blowing, swinging them on the taut rope. Yes. Suddenly a
car draped with a tarpaulin drew up near the street
lamps. A short ladder was fixed to one side. The guard
opened their ranks and a civilian emerged from inside.
He was wearing brown boots and a camouflaged
waterproof, the kind that would merge into the background of fields so that I could never spot him. I think
I might spend a hundred years looking round without
being able to find that camouflaged waterproof. And
there inside me by day and by night, I suddenly see
that man in his field-camouflage move into action,
stretch out towards the first of the hanged victims,
draw a knife from his pocket, cut and saw and finally
release him.

"He was number one, Giotto, the newsagent. He
fell forward with a thud on to the road. The man
mentioned before, in the camouflaged coat, was again
in evidence. Then he descended and dragged the
ladder to the second lamp-post. He was whistling a
tune. He whistled well and without pausing to take
breath. It was a monotonous mountain air that he
whistled as he hacked through the rope that held the
red-haired Angelino. And the latter swung round
naked as they had hanged him except for his short-
sleeved shirt to protect him from the North wind,

turned obstinately with his white belly and limbs uncovered like an uprooted plant.

"But even he was detached at length and the camouflaged waterproof started up a lively trill of satisfaction as it climbed down the rungs. Meanwhile another man had emerged from the car; he was bald. He had lit a cigarette and had sat down on the mudguard, watching. Yes. He cut down Meli, the architect from the new hospital. The body fell on to the macadam. They say he had four machine-guns concealed in his cellar, one for each of the town gates. So had Pino Rosati and his son Giorgio. They had been caught in the act of greasing them.

"I can still see them arriving in their heavy trucks in perfect war formation. It was 6th December. They went up as far as San Prospero and made for the graves and behind the crypt. They dug all round and even displaced a pair of bishops to make sure that none of the graves contained any weapons . . . I had mine hidden away too; who hadn't. But they failed to discover them, and while they were beating the countryside, I was in a panic lest Lorenza should turn up – but in point of fact she didn't. She had spotted them from the valley as their vehicle had slowly wound its way first down and then up the hillside."

It was 7th December, 1944, Alessio told me, at dawn when the Five were hanged. The piazza was empty; it had been cleared by two cordons of militiamen. Patrols had searched the houses that surrounded it. Shutters had to be up; the churches were on no account to ring any peals of bells.

The Dolphin Fountain in the town centre directed its spray towards the white sky and the hanged men had to stare at it permanently as it rose, a sharpened blade. All through the grim ceremony it surged up, witnessing it unflinchingly. But when dawn came and the inhabitants were already crossing the gloomy asphalt overhung by the shadows of the hanged men, the water suddenly collapsed and directing its jet around seemed mad to sprinkle the passers-by, the militiamen on guard and even the Five mentioned who could not get out of its way.

Right and left it darted against the sentries' boots and the closed newspaper kiosk. It shot all over the place cascading into the air. At first hesitant and drowsy then embittered and obstinate the bells pealed out with one accord in the midst of it all. The north-wind had suddenly sprung up and it rocked the whole place.

The Five came to life in the arms of this gale and began to swing. The commandant gave the order that the Five should be anchored by means of a weight tied to their feet; the water supply was to be turned off at once, the bells silenced. No one had any right to send these traitors to heaven and for three days the churches were to be closed; no mass was to be celebrated.

The inhabitants who had come down into the streets

surveyed the platoons of soldiers who were hustling round, carrying out the crazy orders, and few there were who abstained from crossing themselves on seeing the cathedral door barred as it was in the normal way only at night, with a sentry posted at each of its doors.

"So the souls of the Five should remain where they are," the commandant had said.

V

The procession had started shortly after midnight. The town was in darkness; complete black-out was in operation by this time. But a searchlight installed on the roof of the Agricultural Bank in the piazza turned its beam on the black lamp-standards. The Five hanged men looked like locusts dangling from the branches of carob-trees despoiled of their leaves by winter. In vain had the wind changed its direction to try and detach them. A white label flapped on Giotto's breast. They had pinned it to his collar. It bore the words, "I am a traitor".

The sentries paced over the piazza, their woollen helmets pulled round their chins, their hands thrust into their great-coat pockets as they shivered under the winds and screwed up their eyes because of the dust that was being blown from *Le Balze*.

It was corporal Costanzo di Taddeo, a Neopolitan from Torre Annunziata, who had given the alarm. From behind the Cinema Imperiale, the angle it makes with the street that goes down from the *Porta Nord*, he had suddenly seen a row of phosphorescent eyes – green eyes – staring at him about half-a-yard above the level of the ground. His mind had been busy with other thoughts but "By the Madonna" these really were pairs of eyes belonging to a crowd crawling towards him on all fours.

Costanzo di Taddeo shouted "Who goes there!" at the same time levelling his tommy-gun at them. The reply was a bleat, not unlike the moan of the wind during the past hours which had been echoing in his own and his comrades' heads. One bleat followed by another to which a man's voice replied calling out that they were friends. A lantern swung above the heads of the sheep which had meanwhile invaded the piazza and went along bleating louder and louder to the accompaniment of a tinkle of bells behind a sullen ram, with its horns lowered, which was going round and round in its own tracks.

"By the Madonna, couldn't you choose another road?" shouted the soldier.

"No alternative route, Signore corporal," replied the shepherd, twisting his beret, and with his wild, round blue eyes full of vacancy he stared at the hanging cluster and the legend on the breast of the news-agent Giotto.

"No alternative route!" muttered a second sentry. "Is that the way to reply? We're not at a gymkhana, are we!"

"No, in truth," the shepherd had it in mind to say but he could not manage to articulate the words; meantime his flock was spreading all round in bunches, in waves, in great upheavals, surrounded the dried-up fountain and pushed against the grill gates of the silent shops.

"Quick! Clear off!"

A large dog yelped busily under the circle made by the spot-light.

"Clear off!"

The shepherd laid about his flock to shift it off the flower-bed where there were odd tufts of grass growing. They wedged themselves together as they piled up on the steep street, with their heads lowered, beating their hard hoofs on the cold flagstones, rushing hither and thither, cowering or rearing up. The shepherd drove them crying out hoarsely and giving prolonged whistles. The sheep-dog had been beaten off by the soldiers on guard, who after a pause began to march on the square again.

And thus they would have continued uninterrupted to the time of the changing of the guard had not a fresh flock emerged from behind the Cinema Imperiale. This time it turned out to be a herd of white cows, sleepy-looking in appearance but vigorous enough in their pointed hind quarters. They advanced swaying their bells, tossing their heads, slowing down, heavy, pensive, in solemn procession.

The sound of their bells, increasing in volume,

surrounded the Five hanged men for a few moments.
The troops darted nervous glances between the
animals' flanks. Nothing there but a line of quivering udders and a smell of cattle stalls. They were
destined for the Market of the Immaculate Conception,
the animal fair that takes place on 8th December.

"Keep moving!"

They bustled along one behind the other, squeezed
into the alley between the fountain and the block of
the Bank building. The herd was caught momentarily
in the beam of the searchlight – a flock of dolphins in
the sea, suddenly thrown up by the night, urged on
by the cry of the men who kept them on the move,
calling them by name and staring insolently at the
four men on guard. These were already staring at the
corner at the back of the piazza, trying to guess what
the new arrivals for the Market of the Immaculate
Conception would be.

A couple of pigs, a black foal, two oxen, some cages
of poultry on a hand-cart and propped up on a bicycle
with its light out went past.

A cart moved slowly across the piazza. It was piled
high with square packing-cases on which the faded
name of a brand of macaroni could still be read. The
cases now contained rabbits. The driver, walking
alongside, his legs wide apart, cracked his whip that
had a red bow on the lash as they proceeded. It barely
missed the face of a soldier who quickly recoiled, hurling imprecations at the old man. The latter replied

with silence, removed the beret from his head and walked past the Five with a serious and eloquent stare as the wheels of his cart slowly revolved and rattled down the flagstones of the sloping street where the smooth asphalt came to an end.

It was not until seven in the morning that two mounted militiamen barred the traffic with a "traffic diversion" notice. The road was evenly covered with a film of red dust.

"It looks as though it has been snowing blood," observed Costanzo di Taddeo, as he made his way towards the headquarters of the Carabinieri where his troop had been billeted. And he looked about him to dig someone out of a café, or milk-bar that might still be open where he could order a hot drink or a glass of wine. But the iron gratings were up and padlocked; the windows were barred, the doors shut and bolted.

"We are celebrating a feast today," replied a passer-by of whom Costanzo had inquired.

VI

It was the 8th of December. Alessio, shut up in San Prospero, had been refused permission to leave the church until a search had been made. A platoon ransacked it without pause for several hours; hammered, pulled out nails, even levered up tombstones and removed panels from the pulpit and high altar. Enclosed as if inside a diving-bell that had a cathedral-like spaciousness, under the pressure of the dominating wind, here in this place dedicated to solitude, they shouted, bawled, heaved flagstones, and clattered round in their nailed boots like a dawn patrol.

A whistle, a line of doggerel, a laugh, a thud. "Get on with it, Alessio, the girl's waiting for you in the piazza Vittorio Emanuele."

Alessio was leaning forward, driving in nails. He could feel Barbarossa's breath at his shoulders and his fixed, ruthless stare. Evidently he had come with the regiment too. He had not been to *Le Balze* for some time, devout member of San Prospero and assiduous in his visits to it, though he was. The last occasion on which he had been seen there – as Alessio well recalled – had been one Sunday morning in June. Lorenza had hurried along that day to lend him a hand. The bombing of neighbouring centres had interfered with their work and they had had to take down and pack every portable object in the minimum time.

She sang at the top of her ladder like a skylark. She trilled away as she removed the damask hangings and dropped them at his feet. The warm air entered through the empty windows and with shrill cries the swallows occupied the eaves that ran along the outside perimeter of the walls. *Le Balze* stood there arid and still, all was peace on the edge of the landslide and down in the gorge where there was a narrow rectangle of golden corn, thick like a hedge with its heavy golden ears. Far away in the valley the song of the reapers

could be heard. Lorenza replied to one of the verses
of their song from the top of her ladder in a clear
rhythmic voice.

Precisely on that calm day – and how distant it now
seemed – Barbarossa had entered San Prospero to hear
mass which Don Raffaele said once a week. It was on a
Sunday in point of fact.

Don Raffaele was often the only one present to
repeat the mass which old Giuseppe, the verger, had
difficulty in following. From the bottom of the three
steps the latter seemed like an eagle-owl replying to
the call of its mate in springtime.

"So be it," he said, bowing his white pate and
jerked the bell vigorously as if to wake himself and the
absent congregation with an incantation. The crucified
Christ with outspread arms and open eyes stared down
at him, turning the palms of his hands, white like a
lizard's belly and pierced by black nails towards him.

"So be it!"

Barbarossa bowed his triangular imperial beard and
closed his eyes with a sigh. He was followed also by his
militiamen who at a respectable distance also repeated
the same gesture and, closing their eyes, knelt down
in prayer.

"Accustomed from their childhood onwards to eat
of thy Flesh, O Lord, couldst thou, O Lord, if thou
existeth, vouchsafe to me in thy mercy, what their
feelings were while thou sustained them in San Prospero, and more especially the Commandant with the

red beard 'Barbarossa'. He was the most attentive at
Mass, the first at Communion, thrusting his dry lips
forward to receive the Host. As he recited the litany in
a solemn voice and heaved great sighs, wringing his
hands, he implored thy mercy on bended knee."

The militiamen, erect and with deliberate movements, then withdrew from the church, and passed
over the hollow tombs in silence. When they had gone
Giuseppe, the verger, quickly cleared and folded the
lace-edged altar- cloth and extinguished the two candles
whose flames had crackled for an hour above the two
up-turned lizards, and the white palms of the crucified
figure, trembling, twisted alone in an attempt to free
themselves from the pressure of those nails which
had riveted Him so cruelly to the wood for all these
centuries.

"Look," continued Alessio, "they have all gone
away. Don Raffaele took a short cut in the direction of
the presbytery and the swallows began to dart round.
Some entered the windows and darted under the
capitals. The singing of the reapers could no longer be
heard coming from the valley. They must be having
their dinner. And not even Lorenza began to sing
again and I looked for her along by the walls of the
hospital and on *Le Balze*. I finally found her lying on
her back under the high June sun at the edge of the
cliff. Her feet and legs dangled in space and she was
swinging them slowly, absorbed in her thoughts.

" 'Lorenza!' I called, 'come back. The earth is

liable to crumble away at the edges; it is dried by the drought.'

"She laughed by way of reply. 'Let me kiss it,' she said; 'it is my ally; my only ally. It will soon push its roots under your Chamber of Horrors.'

"Have you grasped what she meant? She was calling San Prospero the Chamber of Horrors because of those paintings that recount the story of the martyrs which are to be seen there. I replied to her. 'You're a heathen to speak like that.' 'I, a heathen?' And she stared at me.

"Hers were the uncomprehending eyes, yellow, dilated, of the cat with their expression of mixed horror, innocence and wonder. There was a hardly perceptible flash of anger in them. And she moved forward and in two bounds she was back again, barefoot, and with her light stride was pacing out the long aisles of the church and speaking in an extremely agitated voice. Her small white hands were uplifted in despair and she drummed them angrily against her body, the frail wall of that youthful body, so shaken by shudders that she could hardly move it, and her blood rose in her breast and she almost suffocated. Unreasonable but inspired – that was how she struck me at that moment. Convulsed with rage – that was how she must have appeared in the Piazza Vittorio Emanuele on that sinister morning of the 8th December, unburdening herself of her wrath and calling out to the Five to witness that the landslide was her sole ally against all the rest of us who refused to follow her, against me even, who had not yet understood.

"She rushed down to the piazza as soon as she had heard of the hanging. They say that she ran along the upward slope in the teeth of the gale that was blowing the red dust all round her. They had just changed the guard; the barrier marking the road diversion had been fixed close to the Cinema Imperiale. Lorenza strode over it. She was warned to go back but she had no intention of doing so, they told me. She was looking round her. I know that look, I know what she saw against Rosso and Giotto and their comrades. I know that she was waiting in silence to see it properly, to recognize it – and she saw it again and it was motionless and within it dangled the Five hanged men and within it too marched the four militiamen.

"And this is what it was; what rose in her mind was the whinny of the horse. I am convinced that is what Lorenza saw. And right into the midst of that whinny all of a sudden strode Barbarossa."

VII

She had already told this story but only to Alessio. She had felt compelled to, she said, because not even he believed in her and along with the rest of them persisted in following the cult of torture. For worshipping it in this way in the House of God merely served to perpetuate and spread it.

"Look!" she said.

They were in San Prospero at the time, and it was still June. They were confronting the picture that stood on the altar of the side chapel where Don Raffaele had just finished celebrating Mass.

"Look!"

It was the work of some anonymous artist of the twelfth century painted on a wood panel. A crucified Christ, alone, raised above a green meadow through which a river flowed. Birds were flying above it in the distance. The anonymous Master had peopled the ground with brightly-coloured flowers and insects and a number of frogs. Christ, nailed and naked, rose pale above them on a black cross. His head hung down on his emaciated neck; his ribs stood out as regular and well-defined as iron-railings; his fleshless limbs, yellowed by time, his feet placed one on top of the other and fixed by one nail in the middle, ended in a fan-shape, splayed symmetrically like the notes on a key-board. Gouts of blood oozed from his belly, his spread-eagled arm and forehead.

Magnificent and horrible; it was perfect. Lorenza stood there, pointing it out. Shudders of anger and terror shook her body.

"That is why I do not attend your churches. I find that everywhere on your walls, between door jambs, above candelabras, and doors, above the floor in marble, majolica or bronze, everywhere, suspended thus, tired, emaciated. I find it in colours or in white on the cross

T.S.—D

or bent beneath its weight, now spat on, now nailed up, bloody and naked. Wherever I look there it is in every shape, set in precious stones, made in enamel, in sculpture, in mosaics and frescoes, always stretched above this same instrument of torture on the cross." She spoke without piety in clear tones, pointing at Him, the Lord. And it was Lorenza, herself the tender-hearted pale and incensed, apprehensive yet resolute. A small yet impressive voice came wearily from her thin, skylark's breast.

She had visited cathedrals and churches, she said, and on the end wall of school-halls, above her mother's bed, in post-offices and in lottery kiosks, there He was on the cross. You saw His image scattered about among the fair-booths, given away practically for nothing, roughly carved in cherry wood or cast in silver, gold or lead. Everywhere. On the necks of new-born babes, dangling from the skirts of hospital sisters, on the back of the girdles of priests in processions, swung this crucified form. Or, as at present, in mosaic it surged above the gloomy apse. The chorus that followed him was that of his own martyrs, on foot, solemn, each with his own offering on a plate, a severed tongue, a breast sawn off, a pair of hands. . . .

"Look at these hands, look at them, Alessio! This is only a single pair drawn to perpetuate the memory of them. But when I saw them after the first air-raid they were scattered all over the stubble field and among the sun-flowers, there were so many, some of them severed from the arms, all sizes, they were in piles like daisies, like paper-bags turned outwards with their white palms, swollen like frogs' bellies or clutching at the earth, the backs of them bent round, the veins still strained with the effort of wrenching at the door-handles of the train.

"At that time I was living with my relations not far from the railway signal-box, just beyond the iron bridge."

The train was moving slowly, the coaches gently rocking. To the airmen above it must have looked like a caterpillar slowly and smoothly gliding over a green leaf.

And high above it they spotted it and took aim. They caught it right on the bridge. The girders collapsed, the lines crumpled and the coaches hurtled down below on to the dry river-bed.

Twice the squadron flew over. They returned, still attacking. One man who had escaped uninjured was running along the gravel. He looked like a stray cat or a lamb that has got separated from the flock or perhaps a young bull that had got loose. They machine-gunned him too and the others who scattered like seeds at harvest time, like hailstones that bounce off the roadway.

Evening descended. The sun, still very bright, was sinking in the west. The dogs in the countryside around, chained in their kennels, were barking and a hen was still cackling from her perch while her chicks lingered on in the cattle-shed scratching about in the dung between the animals' legs.

The sunflowers, tired of following the course of the sun, had only just began to nod and it was they, standing there in a kind of hedge that got the first blast.

Down they all came – fragments of debris, some of it human. Toppling down the river-banks, bouncing off the stones among the gravel, sliding off the strawstacks. They lay in heaps, the colour showed them up, flat or hanging as if they had been put out to dry in the early night wind on the trees – pears, holm oaks, from the very top of poplars, flapping and waving like flags that have suddenly been hoisted before the darkness envelops them. They floated in disarray on to the hard stubble-field and trembled for long enough, quivering like the severed tail of a lizard, leaping like newly-landed fish, moving about among the fragments of wreckage, pieces of boiler, pipes, running-boards, buffers.

But when the sun rose again and revealed the scene of the disaster everything had calmed down. The earth was stained red and the silence was broken only by the desperate, continuous whinny of a horse. A horse which, abandoned along with the other horses, lay helpless in the railway truck where it had been shut in at the start of the journey.

They collected up the debris with pitchforks, spades and shovels and removed them in carts and tractors. It took several days to raise the coaches and dig the rocks out of the signal-box, and extricate passengers who were still groaning from the twisted mass of rails and girders. And there was one voice that sometimes was like the braying of a donkey sometimes like a peacock screaming at nightfall.

Lorenza watched them go one by one. She too lent her help. She saw the charred remains of the engine-driver and the fireman who had been roasted alive over the furnace.

"Here he is; look here he is coming back again!" cried Lorenza. "Look, up here in your playground!" And she pointed to the figures in the stained-glass windows of San Prospero. She was drawing his attention to Saint Lawrence at the top who was being roasted alive on a grid. A ray of light was lighting up the coals and from the church roof came the mournful lament of the turtle-doves. The swallows were darting along the cornices once more and the reapers in the valley sang in chorus as they cut the corn and cleared the field.

VIII

"Perhaps you are now beginning to see the origin of my vocation, Signore?" continued Alessio. "She had such fine nostrils, Signore, as sensitive as a fish's fins. She was deathly pale as she told me her story. She said that uttering words was like sowing seeds. The ground was hard and they should not be left to float on its surface; the river was dried up. But the cicadas chirruped patiently and in the river-bed she found snails tucked away inside their curved, striated shells.

"Did she voice her thoughts to Barbarossa when she discovered him in the piazza by the lamp-posts? I shall never know. But what I do know is that he shouted to her to clear off because it was forbidden to pass that way. But Lorenza went on all the same. By this time she had reached the edge of the whinnying – she was walking straight into it.

"Barbarossa accompanied her urging her to be sensible. Then all at once he put his hand to his revolver holster to frighten her. It must have been at this point that Lorenza removed her helmet and showed who she was.

"It all followed its terribly logical and inevitable course, Signore. I keep going over the ground in reverse order to see if I haven't got it wrong somewhere. But the account proves it to have happened exactly as I tell it. Lorenza – it was 8th December – had to leave the farm at six o'clock in the morning. She had slung her wooden sabots from her belt so that she could hurry. The wind was blowing against her as she climbed, making her late. The diversion barrier had been erected at seven o'clock next to the cinema and Barbarossa who had left the barracks by then, had arrived at the piazza to make sure that his orders had been carried out.

"He came in from the right, she from the left and advanced obliquely. He ordered her back. Instead of withdrawing she merely fixed him with her eyes, they tell me, and stopped a few yards away from him. Then in her patient, gentle voice she requested that he should show her his amulet and asked whether he still had the courage to go on letting it hang from his neck on its gold chain.

"Barbarossa did not grasp her meaning and once more he ordered her back. Perhaps town squares were his private preserve, she asked. Centuries ago they, his predecessors, had crucified a man and he by way of preserving the custom and the memory of it, wore the crucifix round his neck. Indeed had she not seen him genuflecting in the building at *Le Balze* to keep himself in practice, and certainly he had fallen on his knees to pray before ordering the execution of the Five.

" 'Stop this raving and clear off,' warned Barbarossa. He had seized her by the arm. But she broke away and ran in the direction of the lamp-posts. I know they were both shouting by this time. Lorenza to replace the sound of whinnying in her ears, Barbarossa to cover it up. Meantime the inhabitants of the houses in the piazza rushed to their shutters, window-bars and doors. This too was logical and significant because when Lorenza flung herself at him, shrieking to him to open his tunic to prove that she was telling the truth, an earthenware jug fell in the neighbourhood of the militia escort. It was followed by a shoe and a pair of boots. . . . Could these be attributed to the wind or had they come from people hiding behind those windows?

"But perhaps it was really and truly a sudden wave of madness that had come over everybody. The militiamen fired in the air and Barbarossa, bull versus gazelle, swaggered into the ring.

"The outcome was now inevitable. The doors, windows and shutters remained closed but objects still continued to rain down on the piazza to the accompaniment of cat-calls and whistles. Lorenza had been tied up and was lying on the ground. She stared round her. The people on the roofs wanted to come to her rescue but she must also have seen the same strange rain coming out of the sky as she had seen at the time of the signal-box disaster. All manner of things were now falling – soup-plates, boots and shoes still warm from owners' feet.

"She lay there flat on her back, silent. She must have been aware of herself floating there with outstretched hands, but this time the stubble-field had turned into an asphalt pavement. Yes, she could see Silvagni the hairdresser's sign in the background; perhaps she murmured his name mechanically as she stared at the balcony situated above the entrance and the 'permanent-wave' advertisement. Baskets of geraniums hung from the balcony; they were not yet in flower, and the green stalks swayed gently in the wind. Across them fell the shadow of the Five. They too were swaying to and fro.

"It was not yet the season of the cicadas or the swallows but the red dust, clotted, covered the expanse of tarmac as it had covered the signal-box. *Le Balze* had sent it to her – it was all very logical.

"It must have seemed logical to her who was always logical to the point of irrationality. Yes; perfectly logical, I repeat. And it was logical too that I should not be there; and I could not be there, for I was being kept a prisoner in the church of San Prospero and I had no idea what was afoot, forcibly detained as I was to carry out repairs on the tombs that they had been opening up.

"Who will ever know if she looked all round before her end to see if I was there?"

"But at eleven o'clock Barbarossa had cried, 'Let him go!' And they turned me loose like a dog."

IX

Alessio continued to talk in calm tones with long pauses between. His lower lip, dry and swollen, obtruded and his eyebrows were raised. He looked round him with those green, steady eyes.

"She stood against the back wall by the hairdresser's sign. Her feet were no longer in contact with the ground and her knees showed their rounded shape beneath her cotton skirt. The Five seemed to have made room to receive her, and they dangled near, rigid but composed. She held her head lowered, thinking of the future and her green, ruffled hair fell over her eyes. The wind shook her, provoking a slight shudder and she seemed to lunge forward. The rope creaked as if it was holding back a boat that was eager to cast off.

"The time passed calmly, almost imperceptibly in the piazza. The sun continued to rise and raise the curtains of night, drawing them carefully. The days, as they say, followed each other; the nights chased them without ever catching them up. I walked about the earth, floating on its surface. I have no recollection of what I did; all I know is that I walked on and on."

Alessio had now been talking calmly for several hours. But on reaching this point, his imagination seemed to take complete charge, and it was a painful business keeping pace with him and extremely difficult to make a coherent account out of it all.

From then on, that is from the time when he himself entered the scene and became a participant – and it must be remembered that he went about suffering from loss of memory for several months – it was as if a clumsy operator with a magic lantern had got his slides mixed up and instead of following in a proper sequence they occurred in any sort of order.

He assured me that he hated fields because they were the hiding-place of the cunning man in the camouflaged cape who climbs up his little ladder in this disguise and cuts down the victims and they fall with a thud on to the asphalt below. He told me that he was never free from mistrust as he wandered across those fields. He often had to climb up a whole row of poplars where an image seemed to be swaying silhouetted against the light. Among beeches, pines, almond-trees and even the dwarf-pears, wherever his glance alighted the bare winter branches seemed to form themselves into a crucifix, as though they were warning him.

He avoided inhabited places and obtained his food from peasants and shepherds who lived in the scattered hamlets of the valley and mountains. They were hospitable and generous to refugees. He told me that he kept his counsel wherever he went, that nobody asked him his name and that if they had he would not have known what to reply. Siegfried? No. His true name had not yet been revealed to him.

He moved among the shadows. They alone resembled what he had lost. But they vanished at first contact and then he had to find others and proceed, step by step, mile after mile. He slept under the trees or in cattle-stalls, close to the breath of animals and shook off his sleep with the first light of dawn. Tree-trunks, grass, ants made up his world; he watched the branches put out buds, leaves and then fruit. He watched the potatoes from when they first flowered, he watched the corn grow up. He saw the Milky Way stretch over the hill-top. He watched the wheat ripen; it was like the river Tiber driven by the wind down towards the river-mouth of maturity. The hoarse frogs croaked round him as he walked among them. He could not remember how many cock-crows he had heard. Always he pushed onward. The grapes ripened and were cut and blind gnats circled in clouds over the must.

He felt no desire to return; he must keep pressing on. But one evening he saw San Prospero confronting him, quiet within its walls rising up from the age-old cliffs.

"It was November by then and evening. It was cold. Eleven months had passed since the time when they threw me out. I could not recollect where I had been; I went my way muttering old songs, and paying no attention to the road I happened to be following. I suddenly noticed San Prospero squatting there, waiting for me and the clock on the campanile squeaked out two o'clock. I raised my head through force of habit and noticed that a weather-vane had replaced the banneret on the campanile. But there was little wind blowing that day. I was the only one disturbing the empty air.

"I raised the knocker but no one came. Anyway I knew how to get in and I entered.

"My first recollection is of a fly which smelt me immediately, for it alighted on my cheek. I was indeed the only source of heat inside that building and the fly, escaping from the first frosts, buzzed desperately round me and tried to crawl into my hair.

"Next, on the ground I perceived the white and shining bib of a snail and the volutes, circles and hesitations of its quiet wanderings. It had climbed above the loftiest memorial, a vast one. Its trail crossed the

epigraph and was lost in the marble pall under the
angel-figure on the right-hand side. Now, I thought,
it is sleeping in the bosom of the departed.

"I recall that I was standing up in the middle of the
building and that the fly had carefully sought out the
back of my neck. I felt enclosed in that ancient silence.
I allowed my glance to settle on the chain of the apse,
and all of a sudden I saw them – I saw them as in a
vision – and I dipped my fingers in the blood of my
Lorenza and all about me I seemed to hear the name
'Siegfried'.

"They rose up by the sloping walls, each had been
frozen in a last, final gesture by an expert hand, a
hand skilled in the delineation of each detail, lovingly
recording this or that aspect of the scene. They ascen-
ded in hosts, in rows, alone, some naked, lean figures,
some with their bright robes gathered about them. The
Flood was forcing them to flee and ascend a mountain
that in parts bristled with larch-trees and spruce and
in others was a stony wilderness. They fled in families
and in small groups; some drove a heifer before them,
some a grey donkey with a straw mattress or a small
barrel on its back. A relentless rain lashed their faces,
mingling with their sweat and tears. The glint of
terror that was in their eyes could also be observed in
the birds that circled above them and the animals that
walked below or pursued each other, thrusting by one
another in their panic and suffocating each other in
their anxiety to escape the rising water.

"Above the transepts, arches, piers – everywhere – I saw this stampede. Cattle were rushing across the mud, some of them falling down, mixed up with wicker chairs, baskets, wooden chests, babies in long clothes. Some of the people were stretching forward from tongues of land, trying to grasp hold of those who were being caught and swept away by the flood. I can see their hands now, some clenched, some open, tiny or huge, all clutching at the grey air. The river is no longer dry, I cry. I am sure I must have uttered these thoughts aloud for my voice re-echoed in the nave as in an organ pipe. 'The river is no longer dry, Lorenza.' I repeat, yet . . .

"They were in line. Each one seemed to be coming forward to take a curtain at that moment, and Saint Eulalia leaned out towards me, holding a tray containing her severed breasts; Saint Andrew, close by, his inverted position suggestive of a juggler, was lashed upside down to the wheel, while Saint Sebastian, leaning against an evergreen oak, offered his bare ribs to his tormentors. One man who had been violently scourged had collapsed on the ground in the double-window. And wheels, pulleys, screws, racks began to move, rocks and metal-rings expertly handled began to descend on the victims again. Oak, elm, ash rods, scourges and whips, balls of lead, finger-nails, iron combs, hemp, wax, and pitch torches sprang once more into life.

"Everything was depicted even on the stained glass

in great detail. How many times, I their restorer, had restored them in their martyrdom, in that exaggeratedly springlike landscape. 'Take them away! men are using these pictures as a school; it has become their alphabet,' I could hear Lorenza whispering in my ear. 'And it was here that Barbarossa came to feed his mind.'

"A Christ stared down at me from the cross. I saw the yawning pit of his belly. And I approached it.

"It was full moon, and I worked all through the night. A termite in the heart of the wood broke the silence at intervals."

X

"No one went up to *Le Balze* during the next few days. It came on to rain. The fly had vanished and as for the glistening track made by the snail I had unwittingly obliterated it with my own footsteps.

"I did not leave the church for fear of being seen. I had enough food in my bag. I set to work assiduously. Over the frescoes, now impossible to remove, I nailed straw mats. In place of the stained-glass windows I fixed boards to keep out the weather. I wondered whether they would do the job or rot before the winter was over. In the more exposed south aisle the windows were often subjected to violent squalls. The rain seeped through, animating the red-hot coals under Saint Lawrence which seemed to glow as though newly kindled.

My careful restorer's hand had trembled nervously as it detached the various fragments. The water leaked through, trickled down the metal grives and lodged among the geometrical panes and figures in the glass which, undisturbed for years, had resisted all my research and curiosity while they were under my care and now, having broken from their moorings looked as if they had come to life again, writhing under the most cruel torments.

"Whether it was the rain or the trembling of my hands I do not know but in the succeeding days in the glass and along every wall I saw snakes gliding again over the shoulders of the kneeling girls, whips thrashing the air and the ground and the bodies of those early Christian martyrs, and wherever I looked in the church I saw a flash of white limbs, a jerk of the bodies to the accompaniment of the lament of the wind, the groans of hinges, the hissing in the cracks of the building.

"Unknown, anonymous, victims so many of them like those of the signal-box tragedy. And while I removed them from the glass an obstinate rain lashed my face.

"It was a slow business – but I carried out my intention, Signore. With the removal of the glass the worst was over. I left the rose window *in situ* because its artist – perhaps to compensate for the others – had depicted an Earthly Paradise inhabited by swans and white doves. And in the same way I refrained from covering with mats, above the aisle arcade, a combat – that between Love and Chastity –

"When I had come to the end of my task, I remember, I fell on my knees. I had opened the central door and I knelt down in the entrance. It was one o'clock in the morning. I recall hearing the clock in the campanile striking once. What day it was I had no idea. I had not kept count.

"It was not raining and the setting moon behind the clouds suffused the *Balze* with its light. I remember hearing the dogs barking in the valley and that the wind, pressing against my sweat-covered shoulders, gave me its serene blessing."

XI

The rest of the story is already known. I was present in point of fact when they caught Alessio red-handed in the church of the Annunziata. Three months had passed since then. Three months' detention for "observation" of his exhausted body.

He was so anxious to get out, he told me on one occasion, if only for a few hours. And he implored me to help him.

I promised to interest myself in his case and in point of fact I put myself to no end of trouble to obtain a permit from the doctor in his ward. I prevailed on Alessio to promise that for these few hours he would call a truce to his activities. We would go out into the country. I would try and hire a carriage.

We had by then got into the first days of October

when with me as guarantor we were allowed to pass out of the gateway. I gave him my arm to support him. He looked round him as if he was drunk and walked on mechanically. He seemed like a blind man who had suddenly recovered his sight. He touched everything that came to hand and before getting into the car he insisted on making a tour of the piazza and caressing every lime tree.

"I would never have believed," he said to me, as we strolled down the sloping roadway, "that it was so easy to burst through the horizon."

We walked across the fields for about an hour. The grape harvest had already begun and the peasant girls were singing in their rows as they cut the bunches. At the edge of a treading floor, some boys were playing on a swing. They had slung a rope between two cherry trees and, by way of a cushion, a verdigris-stained jacket had been folded across it. They were swinging away happily.

Alessio who had stayed silent all the way there suddenly seemed moved at this spectacle and asked me if it was possible to go down a few yards and have a closer look at the boys. I was delighted by his request. We crossed the stream and slowly approached the treading-floor. The boys had seen us get out of the car and had stopped their game to stare at us, full of curiosity. A bunch of little girls was also observing us from the other side of the enclosure. There were half a score of them, all barefoot, varying in age between two and fourteen, and they had all been adorning their heads and clothes with leaves and twigs of vine plants. Some had picked themselves sprays of green leaves, some leaves that were reddening, others that were a golden colour, and these were now draped from their belts like dresses or rose, crown-like, from their foreheads or hung in garlands over their thin chests.

"Look," whispered Alessio, "it is the feast of the grape harvest."

His eyes flashed from one group to the other. The boys had begun swinging once more. A white bitch came up to us, wagging its tail.

"Marcellina," called out a little girl.

"Lie down, Marcellina," cried the girls in chorus.

Marcellina squatted down by our side, or rather, we sat down by *her* side near a pile of wood. The treading-floor extended before us. It was on a slight incline and the boys were playing on the right and left hand side of its base. Some had casually resumed their previous occupation but the girls, feeling themselves under observation were pushing each other about, laughing in high-pitched squeaks. Then as each turned to look at us they started to dance in a ring. We could hear a mandoline pizzicato coming from a stable behind us, punctuated by the lowing of a cow. An atmosphere of calm reigned round the place. A rosemary bush filled the air with its perfume.

Alessio lay on his back with his neck resting on the heap of wood, anxious not to lose a single gesture from these boys as they played. His glance passed intermittently from one group to the other. Marcellina, giving great sighs, turned round in her sleep. A blackbird was running here and there between the rows of children. *Le Balze* were far away and so was the war, symbolized in a twisted, rusty wreck of a lorry leaning against one of the cherry-trees that functioned as an upright for the swing and in the crumpled German sailor cap which one of the boys had thrust on his head.

The vine branches flew round during the round dance and became detached from the dresses. The girls chased after them and fixed them in position again with pine needles. One of them had picked dahlias and woven them in her hair; another, a modern Ceres, had a mass of yellow corn ears dangling from her neck; a third, a little brunette of about six, had even managed to decorate the crepe mourning band on her left arm above her elbow with daisies.

They sang or rather chanted in chorus. When they had finished their dance and seen that the swing was free, they rushed over and began to take turns on it. The boys meantime had posted themselves on the wreck of the lorry.

The cherry-trees creaked in the high foliage. The swing rushed downwards then swooped into the air as though borne on wings. The pause at the top was perceptible and accompanied by gay laughter and squeaks like those uttered by swallows as they skim by the edge of the guttering.

Once again the large vine leaves fell off their dresses and fluttered down, pregnant with autumn. The dahlias and daisies likewise flaked off, the ears of corn rustled down, at the same time shedding their grains. A couple of hens ran up and voraciously devoured the seed scattered on the beaten earth.

The shadows lengthened and the swing, dying down, had weighed anchor in the evening harbour and hardly moved. The girls reappeared, stripped now, except for their cotton overalls, but the excitement of their game still remained in their burning cheeks and their wind-shaken hair. One of them was searching in the grass in the neighbouring olive grove for her comb and hair slides; the brunette with the mourning band came up to us and offered us grapes which we accepted.

"What's your name?"

"Genoveffa."

"And the others?"

"Marisa, Annamaria, Pasqualina . . ."

But "Marisa!" came a shout from over beyond the stable and they all darted off. The boys had already been gone some time.

We went up. The verdigris-stained jacket which, folded, had served as a swing seat had fallen on the ground, and the rope, blackened by its previous use as a bridle, now hung limp between the two cherry-trees.

Night had caught us unawares. The mandoline, the chorus of the harvesters and the click of the scissors among the vine plants had ceased. The only sound was the deep bass lament from the cow.

Carts descended the nearby main road accompanied by the deep voices of the men who had been gathering the fruit and the clop-clop of the mules, laden with large tubs filled with grapes on their pack-saddles, banging together at every step.

"It's the carnage of Bacchus," said Alessio.

His voice sounded confident in the darkness.

"It's a recurring and seasonal affair like all massacres. Blessed are those who, like these girls, know nothing of its origins. They continue to swing happily on the rope of the swing without knowing that this same rope was used for the Five of the piazza – and for my Lorenza."

I was close beside him and despite the dark I saw that he was tugging at it in his hands as if he was trying to pull it apart or untwist it.

I saw too – and it was the first time this had happened since I had known him – that tears of grief were running down his emaciated cheeks.

Marcellina had run up again and rubbed herself against our legs, whining.

"It was Bacchus, you know, who taught the shepherds how to produce wine. And all the stories and even this one begun thus – with excitement or love. And they all, like this one, suddenly turn into disaster. Icarius was allotted a whole cask of wine to sample. They all sampled it, shepherds and the rest of them, without distinction. You can understand how it all ended. A drunken orgy. And that's how it always is, that is to say, Signore, that some get intoxicated on wine, some on ideas and the result is many a massacre. And every one of them, shepherds or not, drunk as they were, of one accord dragged Icarius into their midst and beat him to death. I expect I seem to be digressing here. But you do see, don't you? Look, this is always the same rope that I am holding in my hands."

I was eager to hear his story out, knowing from experience that however high his imagination soared, he would always come back to earth again and pick up the thread he had abandoned. But I must confess that on that evening, up there in the tranquillity of an unfamiliar country I was afraid for a moment that he would lose the main thread while he was digressing and telling me about the drunken shepherds and enlarging on the fate of Icarius and that of his daughter who at the news had become insane and had hanged herself on a branch.

"A cherry-tree, perhaps," added Alessio, "like the one we have seen. For a long time she dangled under the rain, benumbed and alone. She was called Erigone. What do you think, Signore? How old would she be? About the same age as Lorenza I expect. She must have swung a long time at the caprice of the wind and the rain. And it was like throwing a stone into a pond; the rings widen and multiply and soon the other maidens were hanging from the branches, slender and white and small though their necks must have been. It was the vengeance of Bacchus. The maidens of Athens hanged themselves from the cherry-trees one night after the other under the constellation of Scorpio. Then the cherry-trees shed their leaves and the blossom and finally produced their fruit. And so at this new season of Bacchus when he, as inaugurator of the grape harvest, appeared once more, ropes – as this evening – were still suspended from the branches. Harmless and loose they waited ready to be used, and the girls in the district, daughters of country peasants like Genoveffa and Marisa, seeing these ropes, dangling idly, collected them in pairs and knotted them. Chanting in memory of Erigone and all the maidens who shared her fate, they let themselves swing to and fro, bending their backs to raise themselves into the wind, higher and higher as they recovered their breath.

"That is how the swing originated. Even Lorenza, brought up in ignorance as she was, played the game once."

His voice trailed away. The rope had fallen from his hand and waved idly between the cherry-trees. A noisy chirrup of cicadas filled the valley, and from a nearby pond rose the croaking of frogs.

I took him gently by the arm and helped him across the treading-floor. The little white bitch trotted by our side, leading the way. When we reached the stream she stopped and looked at us as we crossed it and climbed into the car.

I started up the engine and we drove slowly towards the town. Alessio did not utter a word during
the whole ascent and I too kept silent. When we
reached the piazza, Oreste bid us good evening from
the front of his cycle-shop.

"Good evening, Oreste," replied Alessio and walked
up to the gate. I followed and I felt I should have to
remind him to remove his finger from the white bell-
push which he was pressing. The gate creaked open.

I can still see him standing there in the opening –
the threshold between two different worlds. He seemed
in doubt about saying good-bye. In the end he could
not manage to get it out. The car headlights lengthened
the shadow of his back in a grotesque fashion and in
the beam, facing us, we saw the face of the porter with
his bright varnished peaked cap leaning towards us.

I heard the key turn twice in the lock. The dark
rust-patinated surface of the gate was flattened under
the beam of the headlights.

I climbed back into my seat. What could I do? My
hands felt empty, my brain tired. The steering-wheel,
moistened by my sweat, slipped inadvertently out of
my hands and seemed to take control. The car advanced wearily over the cobbled slope along the narrow
road. People moved out of the way as I passed and I
had to slow down behind a cart loaded with barrels.

On the piazza a merry-go-round was turning, scattering the strident music of some ancient dance tune.
Beyond the lamps, sprays of geraniums still in flower

trailed underneath the neon-lit hairdresser's sign. Their shadow, projected on to the wall, swayed silently to and fro in a different rhythm from that hammered out by the mechanical organ.

I continued over the piazza, through the *Porta Nord* and up to *Le Balze*. The church of San Prospero loomed out black behind its walls, now well and truly closed in. The weather-cock hardly stirred.

I could hear dogs barking down in the valley. A night bird which I could not identify sent out a lament from the depths of the gully. I walked in the direction of the cry and rushed to the cliff edge. The cry ceased. I peered into the darkness below. The ground seemed firm, but if I poked it with a stick it would crumble into dust and slide away, disintegrate like leaf-mould in a field of turf or an embankment. If you saw it like this, motionless and innocuous, you would find it hard to believe that with Alessio forcibly detained and far away this soil alone bears the message which Lorenza bequeathed to it.

The Bridge

I

IGNAZIO DID NOT NOTICE the garden until he was already in it. He was walking along a gravel-covered avenue. The gravel consisted of fine white pebbles. Two myrtle hedges flanked the avenue in the distance, two hedges somewhat taller than an average man. You could not see beyond them nor could any voice be heard. The day was so clear that it gave Ignazio the sensation of glass. He stooped and picked up a small, round pebble from the gravel, but just as he was about to drop it, something held him back – it would break the glass. Ignazio put the pebble in his jacket pocket. He was wearing neither cap nor overcoat. He could see the blue sky suspended above his head.

The avenue ended up in another myrtle hedge but on the right-hand side a doorway had been contrived in the vivid green foliage. Ignazio stood in front of it and saw a rectangular meadow surrounded by myrtle trees trimmed hedge-fashion like the other. Ignazio crossed the meadow, found a door in the hedge, passed through it and came upon another avenue like-wise covered with white gravel.

Ignazio began to walk along the avenue. He could

hear his own footsteps crunching the gravel. A myrtle hedge hid the horizon from view on both sides.

The new avenue resembled the other but Ignazio had crossed a field to join it. He sauntered along as before and cast his eyes before him to where the avenue came to a stop in a myrtle hedge. Similar to the other hedges and trimmed to the same height, it brought the avenue to an abrupt close. Having reached the end of it, Ignazio halted. He was suddenly enveloped in silence. He saw that there were no openings in the hedge. Perhaps it would be best to turn back, run along the avenue by the hedges, find the first doorway, cross the meadow, pass through the second doorway and emerge into the original avenue. But at that point Ignazio could not remember where he had started from. Whether he could gain access to the avenue by means of a flight of steps, through a doorway or an iron gate, whether in fact there was any door at all, whether the garden was on the outskirts of the city, in open country or in the centre of a residential district, he had not inquired. As he had unexpectedly stumbled on the avenue he might as well continue from there. Up there too a myrtle hedge devoid of openings barred his way back. The hedge which confronted him had grown closer than any normal hedge for despite the brightness of the day no light pierced its foliage. Ignazio thrust first one hand and then the other into it, shook the leaves and branches and managed to squeeze his whole body through it. A hedge, after all was only a hedge. He had to shut his eyes for fear the twigs should damage them. He noted that the myrtle gave off no smell. Daylight was fading behind him.

Making himself small and pressing his eyelids together, Ignazio walked slowly forward. The crackle of breaking twigs was continually in his ears. On the ground was a layer of damp, almost mulched, dead leaves. His jacket had got pulled back and he drew it forwards with a jerk of his hand without turning round. A smell of fungus rose up from the earth where he trod on it. Myrtle was a strange element in which to find oneself buried and Ignazio was relieved to see the end of it almost as soon as he had opened his eyes. A clear light, as dazzling as it had been before shone through the leaves.

A kind of esplanade opened up before him and cautiously, as if he was taking a step down, Ignazio walked into it. It was bordered by myrtle hedges, low hedges which if he had approached them would not have reached much higher than his knees. The white gravel reflected the light. Ignazio noticed a complete absence of shadows and also that the light, although clear and diffused, was less like sunshine than the white glare of headlights.

Here and there in the esplanade statues had been erected. Some turned their naked backs towards him, and some, likewise nude, toyed with a marble bird. A child pressed a goose against its chest as if it was

strangling it. It was in the middle of a flower-bed surrounded by a myrtle hedge and stood on a rectangular
plinth carved with bas-reliefs representing fish and
snakes. It rose up out of a now empty pond. Water
must at some time have flowed from the goose's beak
as the whitish marks on the sides of the grey basin
proved.

On two sides the esplanade was surrounded with
myrtle hedges like the one Ignazio Matteoli had
recently pushed through; the third and fourth side,
the ones facing each other, were shut off by a wall.
Ignazio made towards one of these. The wall came just
above his forehead and by making a slight effort he
contrived to get a view on to the further side. It was
green pasture land but there were no trees or animals
in sight. On the far side the wall, which was more of a
parapet, fell away steeply and a broad, yellow river
ran just below the garden. It was a turbid, sluggish
river. During the few minutes that Ignazio was
staring at it, he saw tables, dead branches and a
nondescript bundle, shaped vaguely like a dog, drift
by. To all appearances the river was in flood. If
Ignazio had wished, as indeed he did, to leave the
garden, he could not have managed it from that side.
He lowered himself down from the wall and made his
way back to the centre of the esplanade.

He was dazzled by the bright light which appeared
to emanate simultaneously from the gravel and the
cloudless sky. He shut his eyes, placed a hand over

them, but the brilliant glare penetrated just the same and gleaming arrows shot through his closed eyes, causing him acute discomfort. He opened them again and made towards the second wall but the statues continued to turn their naked feminine backs on him. Ignazio climbed up on to the wall. He saw the same green landscape and a slow-moving, yellow river beyond.

Both walls were identical in height and colour, likewise the two hedges though they overtopped the walls. Trampling over the flower-beds surrounded by low myrtle hedges which he had no difficulty in striding over, Ignazio hurried towards the wall on the other side of the esplanade – the side he thought he had already explored. He ran to and fro and saw the same river flowing below the garden. So the river embraced three sides of the garden and curved round beyond one of the two myrtle hedges, and if Ignazio, as was his immediate desire, intended to leave the garden, he would have to retrace his steps along the road which had first brought him to the esplanade. The third side, the only one which he had not explored, was also separated from the dry land by the yellow river according to Ignazio's calculations.

Ignazio made for the hedge. It had closed up behind him and he could see no trace of where he had squeezed through. But which of the two hedges was it? The statues were placed symmetrically and turned their backs on both the hedges. The boy who was

clasping the goose over the dried-up pond and whom
Ignazio recollected seeing immediately on his arrival
at the esplanade was identical on both sides – arms
here and arms there with the two geese sharing four
arms between them. Ignazio felt lost. He was thirsty
and exhausted. The idea of squeezing through the
myrtle hedge again seemed utterly distasteful.

He began to stride up and down in front of the
hedge to see if there was any part where it grew less
closely. He walked for a long time. He ran. The light
did not abate. His feet hurt.

It suddenly occurred to him that he had explored
only one of the hedges, so he went over to the other
and began again. If he wanted the river he had only
to climb up on the wall and go down to it. The river
was there, flowing slowly by with dead things floating
on the surface.

Turning his back on the boy with the geese,
Ignazio sat down on the rim of the pond; there was
still no sign of nightfall. His feet were swollen and he
began to remove first one shoe then the other; he
stretched and spread his toes. The myrtle hedge
formed a dark wall before him. He would have to get
through it; if he chose the wrong one, the river which
curved round beyond one of the hedges would cross
his path and he would be back at the esplanade where
the statues were.

Suddenly however he saw a notice on a green-
painted post next to one of the walls. It had previously

been hidden from view. It had something inscribed on it.

Ignazio ran barefoot towards it. It was the kind of signboard used for traffic indications, and on it were the words, "To the Bridge". An arrow pointed the direction.

Ignazio followed the arrow. It led him to a passage contrived between the myrtle hedge and the wall, revealing a footpath which looked more like a path in a dream. He had left his shoes by the pond but without hesitation decided to abandon them although the gravel drove into his already aching feet. He was afraid lest the signpost and footpath would vanish as soon as he turned his back on them.

Once past the myrtle hedge, the path widened out into a road. It was a broad country road bathed in sunlight like the whole district and bordered with myrtle hedges. You could see where these came to an abrupt end and open country extended beyond them on both sides.

Staring ahead, Ignazio quickened his pace. The road continued and he perceived another inscription "To the Bridge" on a plaque like the one in the esplanade. He heaved a sigh of relief. It was the right direction and in spite of the fact that he was bathed in sweat as if he had been caught in a rainstorm he began to run. He was thirsty. Once he got down to the river he could have a drink of its water even if there were dead animals floating on the surface.

Illuminated arrows flashed past his open eyes and

once more he saw "To the Bridge" inscribed on a plaque fixed to a green post on the left-hand side of the road. This time the arrow on the plaque seemed to indicate the opposite direction, that in fact from which he had just come. But he did not dare to stop or retrace his steps. A splinter of glass or a stone had damaged his right foot which was bleeding

"I will find water at the bridge," he said to himself. "To the bridge," he repeated. "To the bridge."

His right sock was coming down. As he stooped down to slip it off he could hear the sound of water. "Here it is," he murmured.

The road went on and he hurried along it. The line of the road seemed to be interrupted on the right. The river must certainly fall away at that point.

"At last," he said, hurrying along a few more yards.

The avenue suddenly came to an end. The river with its yellow, turbid current was down there. But the bridge was not there.

Ignazio halted abruptly. The white road showing clearly against the green countryside continued beyond the river but there was no bridge. The banks were high and precipitous. But the bridge was missing.

The river was broad and Ignazio stopped and considered. It was impossible to descend to the river. Perhaps he should go back? Along the white road, past two signs, one on the right and one on the left, he came to the myrtle hedges . . . A shudder ran down his spine – what, retrace his steps by the route already traversed and find himself back on the esplanade where the statues were . . . ? No, Ignazio cried out.

The river flowed slowly, gurgling in the stolid landscape. Ignazio stood on the edge of the overhanging bank and shivered. He was no longer tired or hot. Opposite him was the other bank, flat, with no myrtle hedges; but there was no bridge to give access to it. The signpost had been a fraud. The bridge did not exist and in his rage he shouted, "Who says the bridge is not there?"

He closed his eyes and moved forward. He threw his arms in front of him. He still continued to shiver with unappeased wrath, stretched out both his arms again and leant forward. His feet remained fixed, his body shot through space, the air whistled past his ears, his outstretched hands clutched at the earth and buried themselves in the grass growing on the edge of the road on the opposite shore.

II

He had landed.

Ignazio opened his eyes. He saw neither the deserted meadow nor the clear light beyond the river. He lay face down, extended his arms and groped round him. He recognized his iron bed and that it was night and he touched a damp wall which divided him from the corridor. Someone passed by out there, cleared his throat, and spat.

The water from the drainpipe in the courtyard was trickling down as usual – clear, drinking water which flowed into the iron guttering along the whole building. Ignazio was thirsty but it was against the prison regulations to leave the cell. Sweat streamed from his forehead, ran down his neck and his belly. His cell companion was breathing deeply, fetching a great sigh with every breath and moaning. A termite was attacking the cell door, patiently drilling a hole.

The esplanade, statues, myrtle hedge, the leap across the river had merely been what he had dreamed in cell 315 of the sixth section of the prison, Regina Coeli where Ignazio, number 510, had now been locked up for twelve months.

Today, within a few hours, he would be transferred to the Fort. As soon as the sun had sunk among the houses, number 510, alias Ignazio Matteoli, would have had to be ready to face the firing squad in accordance with the sentence pronounced by the special tribunal of a week before.

The lawyer had been joined by the medical officer of the ninth ward. Would his client allow him to take specimens of blood and urine for testing purposes . . . ?

"It's not too late to plead 'unsound mind'."

"I'm not going to," said Ignazio.

The termite had stopped its drilling, and the man in the corridor walked by and gave a cough.

What a splendid jump it had been, considering that the river was more than sixty feet wide and fifteen

feet deep at that spot! Ignazio held his hands before
him to see whether he was still clutching the earth
from the bank on which he had landed. But it was
dark, and only a minute amount of light slid under the
door. Number 509 had stopped his wheezing and was
breathing with a monotonous sound like the suck of
the tide.

Ignazio lay on his back, wiped off the sweat which
was making the whole surface of his body prickle. He
stared at the crosses in the window-opening – there
were six of them, three above and three below. Beyond them daylight was dawning; it was only a
matter of waiting. The day of judgement.

Ignazio laughed. A few bars of a military march
were being whistled spasmodically by the man in the
corridor. Cans of naphtha were being trundled in the
courtyard into which despite its well-like form daylight had penetrated already.

The dawning light advanced with silent rapidity
behind the crosses formed by the iron bars. The town
bells were already heralding it one after another, and
the neighbouring factory sirens joined in. San Rocco,
at home, was now lulled in the quiet air and the
chemist was going down to his shop. It had been to
San Rocco that they had taken him to be christened
when the priest named him "Ignazio Giovanni Maria".
But from now on he desired to becalled "Il Ponte" –
"The Bridge", "Ignazio Il Ponte" to distinguish

him from the Ponte Vecchio, the old bridge with a double span against which the water of the river T, like the uninterrupted curses of the inhabitants of T had beaten for centuries.

It was in fact the Ponte Vecchio that was responsible for all the disasters in the district. If the Ponte Vecchio had not been constructed – and it went back to some date B.C. – the present houses would not have sprung up in this wretched spot which had attracted all the fools of the region, like a stool-pigeon, as they say. One after another, houses had ranged themselves along the shore, although the space between the river and the rocky slopes which followed its course was terribly restricted. Because of this limitation the village had taken shape along the corridor made by the river, a river that was impracticable both for navigation and ferry service, served by a solitary bridge erected at the southern end.

In order to cross over to the opposite bank the inhabitants of T had in many cases to make journeys of several miles. Another bridge was imperative.

In vain repeated petitions were forwarded once a year to the capital and the Ministry of Works for a commission to be set up on the spot to inquire into the deplorable state of the means of communication in the region, the inadequacy of a single bridge for the inhabitants of T and the lack of proper embankments along the river which divided the place into two halves and when in flood, especially in the autumn and

spring, wrought continual damage both to property
and even the people themselves.

When the petition reached its destination it was
read and duly filed, landing up in a pigeon-hole
labelled "bridges" on the top of hundreds of similar
documents which came in periodically from other parts
of the country. A reply reached the mayor of T,
signed by the secretary of the minister then in charge
in which he begged to acknowledge the receipt of
"his petition" and drew attention to the fact that the
request could not be entertained because of the
priority which in the present period of time in national
affairs must be given to ministry buildings, meeting-
halls, barracks, and stadiums.

"And in consideration of the fact that your Commune" – every letter wound up the same way – "has
not yet reached the figure of 30,000 inhabitants, the
aforesaid works cannot be entertained. We sign ourselves, Respectfully yours etc."

This reply was discussed for days on end at the
Bowling Club and in Andrea Matteoli's pharmacy.
Ignazio, ensconced behind the chemist's counter,
listened.

He was nine years old at the time and already handy
with a pair of compasses and a set-square. On the
squared paper of his exercise-book he was planning a
bridge for the place and, with it, a mile and a half of
new embankment-wall to contain the fury of the
river. The old people in the Alms Houses should sleep

undisturbed after the vesper-bell had rung each evening. Ignazio had seen them after they had been fished up following the flood disaster, so-called, of All Souls' Day, when they had been swept away, locked in each others' arms. Their bodies had been caught up by the bushes along the embankment, as the river rushed by in the darkness.

The flood had met them on their way from the Alms Houses to give the alarm. The room, situated in the basement, had been invaded by the river. Then the lights had failed in the houses and streets alike. The two old men, it was said, had been swept along the *viale dei Platani*. The streets had been dark and slimy and how they had managed to cling together when the river had sucked them into its swirling bed no one could explain.

The doctor who attempted artificial respiration on them diagnosed, in one case, violent death caused by his fall on the pavement; as for his companion – the one who had been drowned, he must have clung to the dead man, trying to get him to safety on dry land.

The two old men and a third who was drowned in his room in the Alms House, happening to be asleep when the river had rushed in, were buried together, at the Commune's expense, on the fourth day of November.

It was during the night of the fourth that the river rose in Ignazio's bedroom for the first time. He had gone to sleep late, shaken by the events of the day – the funeral of the old men from the Alms Houses.

He suddenly seemed to hear in his sleep a sound of rushing water and at the same time the iron bed-spring began to rock with a creaking noise and the iron legs which supported it quivered.

Ignazio, opening his eyes, saw the river.

The rising waters were now on a level with the mattress and surrounded the bed on all sides; his shoes had remained at the bottom but some sheets of paper and a newspaper were floating about on the surface. Just then a subdued gurgle issued from the low drawers into which the water was rushing. The river was exploring the room with its liquid hand and Ignazio suddenly realized that he was the one it was after.

He sat up in bed and watched. The water was calm and gleamed all round him. Outside the rain was beating a tattoo on the guttering. As he heard it, Ignazio thought how this collected water was conveyed in the pipe which ran along the outside of the house and how in an orderly fashion it made its way after every rain-shower into the network of drains which stretched away under the asphalt of the road. At this hour of the night the street, the gutter and window were illuminated by a lamp whose light passed through the venetian blinds and flooded the room with brightness.

As the water found its level and filled up all the spaces it ceased to gurgle. The clock of the San Rocco steeple began to strike. Only a few times however.

Dawn was still distant. The lamp kept swinging, making the water quiver on the pavement. The rain, lashed by the wind, beat gaily against the shutters.

"If it rained inside here," murmured Ignazio, "I could speak to the chemist down the drain-pipe in my own room. When I become an engineer . . ."

Ignazio gave a start and his trousers slid off the foot of the bed into the water with a splash as if a frog had dived head first into a pond. Rings formed round the fallen object and widened until they reached the furniture, the walls and the door. If he could reach the door, pressing his hand on the door-handle, the river, caught in the rear, would plunge backward down the corridor where the stairs were.

It wasn't a great distance, certainly not more than five yards. The water however was bright and uninviting. There was none of the mud the river normally had when it was in its own bed. The hexagonal tiles, a white one surrounded by five red, gleamed through, motionless, and next to a chair, the shoes Ignazio wanted to put on stood full of river water. Standing on the bed Ignazio bent forward to tuck in his pyjama trousers. The mattress shook as he took a long stride on to the nearest chair. At this juncture, by dint of leaning forward, he managed to grasp hold of the stool in front of the table. With a chair and a stool the bridge to the door was made.

Gaining the stool, Ignazio got hold of the chair on which he had just passed, stood it in the water in front of him and found himself in the middle of the room. His head touched the glass beads which hung down from the extinguished chandelier.

The surface of the river was covered with rings which distorted the pattern of the tiles as they widened. Once again he pulled the stool in front of the chair, stepped on to it and repeated the process twice until he reached the door. Ignazio stretched out his foot, looked at the handle, the brightest point in the room. He felt for it with his foot. He wobbled and then tried again. He bent forward, his foot swung in space, and, feeling he was on the point of losing his balance, he raised his hands to try and get hold of the chandelier. But the latter hung rigidly down from the brass chain behind him, out of reach.

Suddenly he found himself lying at the bottom of the river flat on his belly with his eyes closed and his arms stretched out. The river-bed was soft. With a great effort Ignazio struggled to the surface and began to swim.

It was still night, the water was calm and Ignazio had not injured himself in his fall. It wasn't cold; indeed the water was warmer than the night air. He turned on to his back, opened his eyes and saw the darkness slowly brightening above him, giving way to a suffused whiteness. The river gurgled gently round him, embracing his whole body. He let himself drift with the current. The water flowed over him, sweeping him along with it. It enclosed him, pursued him, lapped against him, tickled his neck and armpits, choked him with its liquid blanket, seeping through his pyjamas and vest which he wore next to his skin.

But for his anxiety to escape from its clutches Ignazio would have fallen asleep again. The water was assailing his ears with a hollow and persistent roar and its agreeable warmth increased his somnolence. The sky above, with its fleecy white clouds, was gradually becoming brighter, heralding the approaching dawn when all of a sudden a sheet of water rose up behind him and submerged him. A kind of tidal wave lifted the surface. Ignazio slid over on to his belly and as he struck out with his arms on the top of the water a fresh wave pitched over him. He realized from the white foam that surrounded him that, in spite of the raging current and seething waters that lashed at him mercilessly, he had regained the surface.

Now the river bore him along with increasing speed. Exhausted, Ignazio managed to get occasional breaths of air in the midst of the troughs and whirlpools that swung him hither and thither, now sucking him down to the squelchy bottom, now cutting against his face and neck like the cold lashes of a whip.

He must certainly be on the edge of a shoal or of one of the banks; that would explain the anxiety of the river to keep him under before he should get some sort of hold. The darkness into which he had plunged once more had removed any faith he had had in the approach of dawn. What was worse the fits of nausea which came over him were becoming more frequent and warm, bitter water kept trickling from his mouth as he was seized by a sudden chill. His pyjamas and vest had worked their way off his back in the struggle.

Overcome with a sudden faintness he decided to shout for help but his voice was lost among the roars and lamentations of the river.

"Help!" he called out repeatedly but the waves choked him and his gasps became more and more desperate.

"Help!" he shouted over and over. Meantime his eyes, blinded by the river water and his tears, stared into the darkness. No answer came to his cry and for a long time he saw no sign of assistance as his eyes roved round in a panic. Just as he was on the point of losing both strength and hope a dark mass that seemed to be walking on the gliding surface of the water rushed towards him. It was blacker than the night and plunged on to the river. Ignazio could hear the roar the river made as it struck against it and again, for the last time, he gave a terrified cry for help.

For a second the black bastion halted, gathering itself for a premeditated attack. The sky had cleared, the river was white with foam. With a sudden, silent leap the black wall passed to the attack. Ignazio raised his arms to protect his face; the heavy mass – which proved to be the central pier of the Ponte Vecchio – stooped over him and struck him.

Oddly enough he was unhurt. Perhaps the bridge

had moved aside at the last moment, for Ignazio became conscious of a gust of fresh air which caused him to open his eyes.

He was surrounded by a bright light. He was where there was no more rain, beyond the river. By the light of the street-lamp he could see walls rising up round him, cut off by a ceiling. In the back wall was an opening, filled by a double-door; a pair of shoes lay on the floor of what turned out to be his own room, and there was no trace of any water.

Night dragged by endlessly. Ignazio did not manage to get off to sleep until after the milk-cart had gone past the gate.

He had remained on the alert, listening for sounds at the door and window, fearing lest the river should once more try to burst in. The tumefied faces of the old men from the Alms House haunted him, keeping him awake and alert. Up there above the desk where the photograph of his grandparents had been they stared down at him until it was morning. As soon as light from the street-lamp was supplanted by that of the dawn, the grand-parents resumed their accustomed places in the gilt frame, banishing the forms of the drowned old men.

The sound of the whip, bell, and milkman's horn lulled Ignazio to sleep again shortly afterwards and Adelaide had to call him several times, shaking him by the arm to bring him back to consciousness and inform him that it was past eleven o'clock and that the bath, almost filled, was all ready waiting for him.

It was Sunday. The rain had stopped and the day promised well. Perhaps it would be possible for him to cycle as far as the Observatory of R to see the flooded plain. He knew it well. The river had the habit of bursting its banks between November and February but never in all his nine years of life had he seen a flood like this last one. Never had the water risen as high as his bedroom on the second floor of the turret.

Immersed up to his armpits Ignazio carefully soaped himself. He was glad it was day. From now on he would always leave the door on to the passage open. Caught in the staircase-well the river would cascade down the stairs and his parents would hear it roaring and come and rescue him. The river wanted to submerge him. Swollen to grotesque proportions he would be carried away by the current, decomposed and rotten, along with the tree-trunks, wooden posts, and torn-off vine branches.

Although the bath water was hot Ignazio kept shivering. A trickle of hot water ran from the tap, scattering the soap-suds on the surface. He was lathering his face and had closed his eyes, but as soon as they were shut he was seized with a sudden panic. He saw in the darkness the scene he had witnessed during the night. A further thought struck him; the water in which he was now immersed, naked, was the same which ran in the river and which, filtered, served the town for everyday use. The cursed river had sought him out and found him again. It was slowly rising round him, using the pretext of his weekly bath to do so. It was warm as it had been a few hours before when it had marooned him in his bed and had roared round him with its monotonous gurgle and had tried to catch him in his sleep and dash him to pieces against the Ponte Vecchio.

Horror-stricken at the memory Ignazio leaped to his feet. The blue water splashed against the enamel sides of the bath. The black plug stared at him from the bottom, fascinating him. He had only to pull it out and the river would be drained off again. But where to?

Down the drain, into the sewers and from there outside the town and back into its restless river-bed again.

Should he throw it back to be revived again? No. He must punish it; take it prisoner; dry it up; set it on fire if it was possible to set light to water.

Ignazio cast his eye round for weapons. Meanwhile the water continued to trickle from the tap which was still turned on. Now standing up in the bath he shivered but it was so light that he was no longer afraid; far from it. He glared at the water round his feet and spat into it, once, twice, several times. The white saliva floated, moved in the direction of his legs, then dissolved. He spat again and the saliva eddied round his legs which were immersed up to his knees.

"It's making a fool of me!" he murmured.

He raised one leg, let out a kick at the mass of water which swayed and splashed over the rim of the bath. He then raised his other leg and kicked out again. The water spurted up against the polished sides of the bath. More and more worked up Ignazio began to kick out more violently. His clothes on the stool, dressing-gown, mirror, adjacent window, walls were soon drenched with water which seemed to share the boy's rage as he splashed it all round him.

His body, blue with cold, was shivering, but he continued to strike out with his arms and feet. A trickle was running along the floor towards the glazed door. Ignazio spotted it and suddenly it stopped. So that was it; the river was trying to escape his wrath!

"I will kill you in here," he shouted at it. "This time you shall not escape me."

He knew that once water was motionless it was dead.

"You will see; I shall kill you in my house and I shall watch you die and decompose. At present you are alive, white and violent because you are free. I shall keep you a prisoner as long as I want."

The water had calmed down beneath him and it had stopped trickling from the tap. Supporting himself by holding the rose of the shower-bath, Ignazio climbed on to the edge of the bath, which was slippery with soap and water, straddled his legs on either bank of the river. The water stayed motionless below. When Ignazio spat, the spittle fell vertically and stayed where it was without moving. The soap had formed a white scum on the surface and his nail-brush which had sunk was lodged near the black rubber plug.

"It will soon be covered with sedge," muttered Ignazio, "and I'll hear the frogs croaking from my bed. If you attempt to flee at night, I shall be here and stop you, cost what it may. I shall stand sentry over the bath."

He moved over to put himself on guard. He let go of the rose of the shower-bath which he had been holding with both hands up till now, to keep upright. First one foot slipped off the edge, then the other and the "bridge", having lost its balance, collapsed with a crash into the bath.

Adelaide ran up at the cry he let out and found Ignazio immersed in the now chilly water, crying. There was evidence on all sides of his sustained struggle with the water. The walls were streaming, his clothes were soaked. Adelaide enveloped the boy in a bath-towel, rubbed him down and shouted to the chemist to run up with a first-aid outfit to dress the wound. In point of fact the boy's back was cut where it had knocked against the tap. Ignazio had a fit of trembling and was weeping quietly. At intervals he muttered the word "river" and "don't let it get away".

Adelaide asked "who" was not to get away.

"The river," Ignazio replied.

"What river?"

"Ours! It wants to get hold of me, carry me off, as it did Agenore Spoto, to that bush," murmured

Ignazio. "Leave it to die there in the bath. Leave it. Otherwise it will dash me against the bridge. Now that I have managed to trap it, I must kill it. It caught me while I was making a bridge while I was watching it to see it didn't break away again and run along the passage as far as the stairs. It wasn't content just to carry off the old men of the place. I must stop it, father, stand sentinel on the shore, stand over it day and night like a bridge. Once the water stands still it will stagnate and die and you will be saved and I won't be caught in the night and swept away from you."

When they took Ignazio he had recently completed his twentieth year.

They came for him just after midday on the eve of the August holiday. Four police officers in civilian clothes in a black car.

"It's for an offence against the security of the State," whispered one of the officers to the chemist. The young man had to go off with them.

The warrant for arrest was in order. They showed it. The house search lasted until two o'clock. The chirrup of the cicadas sprawling on the plane-trees by the river bank reached the open windows while drawers were being ransacked and their contents collected in two brown fibre suitcases.

At intervals one of the police officers read out the headings of various manuscripts and innumerable typed documents taken from the desk.

"Concerning public works or the future of the modern state; Development league of the South; Irrigation of the district of T, reports and future projects; A candidate's proposal for the reorganization and rationalization of the road system in the Southern Provinces; Statistics of the damages suffered by certain provinces through the centuries – and particularly in our own time – to flood works and concerning the neglect on the part of the Government; Concerning the systematic exploitation of water power; Four questions from the people to its government; On freedom of enterprise; On infringements of liberty and tyrannicide . . ."

"Plenty of good material here, young fellow," remarked one of them as he gutted the mattress and pillows of Ignazio's bed. "Enough here to land you cold at the Fort."

Even the project for the works along the banks of the river T was thrust into the two suitcases; together with the plans for the new bridge. But a copy was left behind at the designer's house.

"Look after it," Ignazio managed to whisper to the chemist on their way downstairs.

It was the 14th of August. The roadway was bedecked with banners and red standards in preparation for the Assumption Day procession.

"I trust that these flags will bring you good luck," mocked one of the police officers, turning to Ignazio as the car slowly moved over the Ponte Vecchio.

"But red stands for blood, young fellow – in dreams and also with us at Police headquarters."

III

To Signora Adelaide Fiori Matteoli,
Lungofiume dei Secchi,
T.

Dear Signora,

I propose with this present to introduce myself, Egisto Cartoni, son of the late Emilio, now residing at number 74 in the via del Governo Nuovo, Barber by profession, being in the service of the Government prison, Regina del Cielo.

Signora will, I know, forgive my style of writing but I left school at thirteen to become a Shop-boy and I have given very little time to Letter-writing except for my period of service as a Soldier in the Province of Rieti, and my Luigina, then my Official fiancée, was at that time in receipt of many letters from me about my Health and Welfare.

But I consider it my Duty to write to you as a relation, namely Mother of prisoner number 510 whom I had the Honour to serve as a Barber in the above-mentioned Government Prison during his period of detention which as Signora will know along with further details lasted more than a Year of Grace.

During his twice-weekly visits to Room 15 which is

reserved for the Barber's establishment, I had oppor-
tunities of entering into conversation with your son,
the late Ignazio Matteoli, during the said period of
almost a whole Leap Year, and I propose, Signora
Madre, with this present to tender you my services as
"Barber friend" and, as Ignazio used to call me,
"Foreman assistant" or that was what he nicknamed
me, he the above-mentioned whom we all knew as
"Il Ponte" – "the Bridge".

I must tell you that Room 15 can only accommodate
three persons (seated) including the one whose turn it
is for a shave and one standing, the latter being
myself the above-mentioned Egisto. But I repeat, when
Ignazio expatiated on his theme in the aforesaid place
we all agreed that it was as if we were facing where a
river flowed past – even when there was no water
trickling from the gutters or from the clouds or the
adjacent taps in the water-closets.

And it is with some surprise that I find myself
today endeavouring in these inadequate words to
describe what Ignazio meant to many of us who
began by jeering at his convictions or described him
among ourselves as a fever-victim living in a continual state of Delirium. And indeed such was the
Document which we drew up in the form of a manifesto signed by some of the attendants of our Division
of the Prison when we saw the official Notice that
Ignazio had to be shot, having been found guilty of
Subversive activities detrimental to the Government,

namely that Ignazio was a sick man in a Delirium and that the causes of the said illness, akin to the madness of the neighbouring Lunatic Asylum, should be inquired into – Signora will excuse our presumption – perhaps a hereditary disease in his distinguished Family. The manifesto was initiated under my signature and it was that which earned me six months' suspension from the Office of Barber in the Government Prisons and Reprimand with attendant fine.

It is not of this however that I wish to speak but of the time when Ignazio entered the aforesaid Shop number 15 and of the subsequent Events.

It happened that Ignazio drew our urgent attention not to the Front wall with its iron-grey Dado but to the Level at which he said the waters start to rise at night when there is no wall there on guard and when the first warmth of Spring melts the snow on the mountains – invisibly – but always pressing in the Background and threatening the Alms Houses or even in the Prison cells near the River, because, on account of the neglect to provide proper embankment walls, the water would overflow the banks and the old men's Corpses, he said, would float round the cellars in Scores.

Signora Adelaide, he had seen them, he says in their flannel pyjamas and with their swollen faces after they had been fished up with a net outside the village where they had been swept away by the river. How many, I asked? Three in one go, he replied. But one was caught under an iron bedstead and they don't float. There he lay held down, covered with green Slime, the whites of his eyes showing and his teeth set in a Snarl. The one huddled up in the patterned bed-cover, under the rusty mattress must have cried out until the water had finally suffocated him and had then fallen Silent.

That is what happens in the absence of embankment walls and the embankment walls won't materialize while the town remains outside the Road system and the Road system does not function unless the river banks are populated and there are bridges wherever they are required.

And this is what he always aimed at, having "his Bridge".

If I looked at him in the mirror he stared back at me with wild eyes that shone Brightly out of the lather which I was applying to his cheeks.

Signora, I know the Story of the Bridges and now I know their necessity as a link between the two shores and their value for the Progress of us men of the present day, and if I were not a Married employee with a baby still in long clothes I myself, Signora Adelaide, would run along the Embankment to rid myself of the haunting voice of Ignazio, he the first Bridge known by me to have come down to this Earth in the form of a man to give us an account of the Benefits to be enjoyed through the proximity of a Bridge or, conversely, the disasters which we should encounter –

and which in point of fact overcame him – if the place was Deprived of bridges, divided and Strangers as we should be, each on Separate sides of the river.

Shaving was a lengthy business when he got talking. Despite my comparative Youth, my hand would frequently begin to tremble as it passed over *"Il Ponte's"* warm cheeks. And when at night the sultry air weighed down on us in Bed, my lawful wife, Luigina would shake me to stop me groaning as I turned over and over in the sheets and reciting the names of bridges – the *Ponte Santeustachio*, the *Ponte Sangiacomo* and that of the *Regina del Cielo* close by where we are now. I would wake up and sit on the edge of the bed.

The Attendant of the Seventy-fourth, Mario Badiali, and Attendant number 12 of the Second Section, Anteo Villani, and the male nurse of the First Ward, Carletto Guidi, whom we nicknamed the Coffee-house keeper, say that sometimes the sweat fairly poured off me as if I was being crushed down by the pier of a bridge weighing down on my bare chest like a Drop-gate, and that they too had suffered from the vague presentiment of their own chests yielding beneath the pressure of a Bridge that grew in their minds like a monstrous Plague, and also of running on to their window-ledges during rain-storms to see that the parapets were resisting all right. All this, despite the fact that the river has been flowing past this city for centuries but has never risen above the

normal flood Level as officially marked on the gauge
according to each season and visible to the naked eye
of every passer-by.

If I tell you all this, Signora Adelaide, it is not with
any intention of digressing from my account but to
communicate to you how the words of your late son,
Ignazio Matteoli, roused in us, his Prison attendants,
an emotion which extended beyond Shop number 15
to the place where I lay in bed with Luigina, our first-
born, Arturo di Egisto, by her side.

And under the influence of the impact of the
memory of Shop number 15, I myself went so far as
to declare one afternoon hardly ten days ago, under
the inspiring words of Ignazio referred to above as
"Il Ponte" – the Bridge, what I would wish if the
Holy Roman Church did not forbid it in its tenets,
namely that I would like to turn into something that
would be of Use to the town if what I believe – the
Resurrection of the Body and Myself – and after I
Egisto Cartoni and my Son and my Wife Luigina are
dead, did not materialize.

But the fact was that Ignazio started it. He declared
himself to be "the Bridge"; of that we were aware.
It was on one sultry day with no West wind blowing
and the swallows were half choked as they squeaked in
the Courtyard of number 5. The men, lean from their
diet of undigested and indigestible greens, had assembled for eight o'clock to be shaved by my cut-throat
razor. The rumour had already been on the go for

three days that Ignazio Il Ponte had to be transferred
to Fort C. I frequently feel a great distaste for my
profession in Prison and the sight of young men with
wide-open eyes staring at the yard. One prisoner, it's
a month ago now, even went so far as to make himself
a pair of Ears of cardboard in the shape of megaphones
to catch the distant sound of the radio beyond the
curtain wall which turned out to be the family Civiero's
four-valve set. And these Ears were able to catch the
sound of Ballet music or snatches of Opera during the
interminable afternoons in those Cells for two. It was
prisoner Arrigo Bechi, a baker, now nicknamed the
Donkey because of his cardboard Ears which he had
to jettison and do a week's "solitary".

What I am driving at is this — I hate the whole
business here and I often manage to slip someone a
letter that I have kept hidden in my sponge-bag,
despite the fact that now and again Searches are in
stituted and if you're caught you are punished by Dis-
missal from Prison service for the rest of your life. I
was keen to study, Signora, but I was obliged to keep
my Mother in her old age along with a young sister
and a Father — who was paralysed — in a Home on the
outskirts of the Town. I enjoyed my work at school,
had plenty of friends; but I had to give it up and
become an apprentice to an Uncle who kept a Barber's
shop. At the thought that my son, Arturo, won't have
a chance to do proper studies, a shudder runs through
me as if I was one of my own poor prisoners.

And they asked me at that time what I should like to be. Are you joking, I asked. Maybe, maybe not, Annibale replied. *His* choice was the railway with its metal lines that gleamed alike in sunshine, rain or moonlight, running through the fields and holding up herds of cattle and everything else at the level-crossings. My choice, I said, is to be a School in the town. A spacious, three- or four-storied School with desks in every classroom. A School for boys, with Arturo among them with his White collar and Promotion stripes mounting up on his left sleeve.

Can't you imagine it all, Signora? I saw it then, and may the Lord and his Mother the Holy Virgin Mary forgive me and also Holy Saint Anne whom I venerate particularly and Theresa of the Holy Infant Jesus.

I could see it all — with its green window-blinds, its rain-washed red bricks, some already weather-worn, with a throng of Children scampering down the main Corridor, kept in order by a fat little janitor. For a moment I even felt their feet running across my belly, coming from every direction, it seemed, with their hob-nailed shoes of every shape and size, although I am not fat. It would be wonderful to be a School, I said, but I do not know how to set about it. If I did, I would give up shaving people. Ignazio said that luckily for schools and Future pupils they were not all feeble as I was. Castles in the air, I said; we pay the taxes, the Government can provide the schools for our

sons, even those of the "have-nots". But you can'
learn how to become a Wall through religion. Ignazio
said, But I'm here to show you how. A Wall, Signora.
What does it matter whether it's a Wall or a School or
a Palace? At the present moment, said Ignazio, you're
merely a good foreman, adept, I may add, at lathering
the Wall you find in front of you!

I shaved him then. That long, lean face of his –
longer and leaner than the face you knew. They say
that he rarely ate and slept very little. Why, Signor
Ignazio, I asked? Because I don't need to. You'll
break down, I said. All right, see for yourself, he
replied. A Wall, Embankment or the Arch of a Bridge
don't need food; they never sleep when lights wander
over them like lovers. He was quite right if he was
thinking about Bridges or whatever it was, but could
I really believe him apart from that particular afternoon when my breast swelled with the desire to be
a School for Arturo – and in retrospect for myself –
forced as I was to shave your son who was condemned
to Fort C from which no one has ever yet returned
Alive? Meantime I stood staring at Ignazio. And he
said, Egisto, why are you trembling? When the
Bridge stands in front of you and you find fault with
it, you must attribute it to your bad workmanship,
Foreman Egisto. And if I had not been tough and
afraid of looking ridiculous, I would have broken
down at that point. Yet he invited me to the Fort.
Come along with me, he said, and you will see – unless

they bring dynamite with them – how astonished the Sergeant who is bold enough to give the firing order will be. You can't finish off a Bridge with a volley of rifle bullets, or even machine-gun fire.

It was at this point that I started on my journey. A dusty uphill road and then a plain covered with much withered grass. I was in the car behind the prison-van with my eyes continually fixed on its number-plate. I shared the vehicle with Don Vincenzo, the chaplain; Ignazio had refused to see him right up to the end. No, Ignazio had said. No, your Reverence, I have no need of you. You would send me to Heaven . . . spare me that, he said. My flight thither will not take longer than crossing from one river-bank to the other. And although I shan't receive a diploma for saintliness, I am none the less capable of crossing the water. He gave a laugh. He often laughed that last day because he said that afterwards he wouldn't be able to or only when earthquakes, rare in his part of the world, provided the pretext for a sudden shock of some kind. Don Vincenzo asked him if he didn't wish to take Communion before being marched off but Ignazio replied that for him there was only one way of communing and he was familiar with that already, along with all the other means of communication in the region – Roadways, Bridges, subways and tunnels. And that he had been studying it all and had noted its weaknesses during the time of his youth now approach_ ing its end and that his present Adventure was con_ nected with the Deficiency of our means of Communication in the whole of the country generally and in his Birthplace in particular and that this deficiency arose from the ignorance of the government which preferred the luxury of marble staircases to the Embankment wall by the river T where it is forced to overflow and the buildings along it to collapse with alarming rapidity.

Don Vincenzo said that Ignazio told him that at the special Tribunal they suggested that if he could hold his tongue in Future and submit to the orders issued by government proclamations he would get off with not much more than Ten years' Imprisonment. But he replied that only in the bridge would he be silent. After all, said Ignazio, talking is not the function of the Bridge which I am in the process of becoming.

Don Vincenzo told me this while he was reciting his Rosary by my side and added that he had asked Ignazio if perhaps he wasn't suffering from a fever. Whereupon Ignazio shook him by the hand and dismissed him. Come and touch me afterwards, Reverend Father, said Ignazio, and you will see how cold I shall have become and how the Marble will slip under your fingers. He is right, he is saying what was in Don Vincenzo's mind namely that he knows he is to die. And, Reverend Father, if you are not afraid, you can pass over me and you will see that I shall not let you fall. Trample on a dead man, someone who has been murdered? Don Vincenzo shuddered but the other laughed. I will transport you to the other bank and you won't get wet, he said. But the Blood . . . What Blood, he asked. I did not say "yours, Ignazio", because he suddenly seemed to have forgotten.

And Don Vincenzo crossed himself repeatedly as we went along the road and read prayers in between times in his Mass-book, those for the Dying and especially those whom he called the Demented. And he asked me how long I had known the Prisoner and that he must be mentally ill or in a Delirium. But I kept silent and I say that even then I did not confess that after the Day which I have called the Day of School I had already begun to believe in your son's Ignazio's powers and a kind of doubt remained in my mind as to whether I was not behaving badly in just shaving prisoners instead of taking part in some enterprise for constructing – each person making something that we require, for everything will be made by our own hands almost without the help of God's grace and of our Governors who haven't any poor sons in *their* families forced to take jobs as employees in a prison, even if it's in the one dedicated to the Blessed Virgin of the Heavens.

But I kept silent about this matter with Don Vincenzo and we reached the Fort C without exchanging any further words. The motor-car engine stopped at the sight of it, like-wise the car-doors and only we ourselves entered the Fort. I was asked who I was And I wanted to cry out, raging at the guard, don't you know me yet, I'm his Foreman Egisto. But instead I stayed silent and showed my Passport instead. Go in, they said.

The courtyard is a huge place with eucalyptus trees at the sides swarming with chirruping cicadas. There was a chair in the centre, it was made of Yellow wicker-work and a piece of rope dangled by its empty seat. The sun beat down relentlessly and the platoon was already formed up in two ranks waiting. Ignazio was the only one in civilian costume except me, and he asked for a Drink which they produced. Then Ignazio objected to sitting down and they granted his request but they said that if he attempted to escape he would be shot down like a Dog. He replied that he had no wish to run away and that steadfastness is in point of fact one of the properties of a Bridge and that being a Dog wouldn't be any use. Then he asked to be allowed to remove his shoes and not to have his eyes bandaged. Then the cicadas sang more loudly than ever from the trees. The rear of the file was brought up by Don Vincenzo who advanced, crossing himself all the while. Then Ignazio pointed to a corner where a long box made of nailed planks was lying on the withered grass and from which emerged a heap of wood shavings, and he said, I see that you have only brought one box and I think that you have already placed the dynamite that filled it under my chair, Sergeant. It's never had dynamite in it, said the Sergeant; the rifles of the firing squad will do the job. I'm afraid that you will vent your fury by kicking against it but you will never succeed in shattering the Marble. Don't you worry, said the Sergeant. We'll manage.

I am now trying to remember every detail because I promised to report it all. The Sergeant consulted the watch he had strapped on his wrist. A Medical Officer ran his hand over Ignazio and pronounced him alive and in a fit state for the execution.

Then the Sergeant asked the condemned man whether he wanted to speak to the Chaplain. No, said Ignazio but, if you allow me, I would like to know your name. Then the Sergeant clicked his heels and stood at attention and introduced himself, Sergeant Major Igino Fedeli. Ignazio extended his hand to him. I am anticipating, he said; but my name is Ponte Ignazio Matteoli. Give the order to fire, Sergeant!

I expect it's all over now, I thought, and looked at the soldiers drawn up in file like a row of steel studs on a pedestrian Crossing and likewise at regular intervals. The Sergeant Major held his sword drawn and I remember that Don Vincenzo called upon the Lord to open the Gates of Paradise. After that I can't remember very clearly in spite of all my Efforts whether he cried out before or after the command "fire". Cowards, he shouted, you did not even bring machine-guns and don't you see that it is Marble, Carrara marble, as smooth as if it came straight from the hands of an expert barber? These were the words I heard or perhaps thought I heard. And the roar of the water will beat against your ear-drums like a whirl-wind, but you must resist, my Friend, cried Ignazio, even though you are immersed in the river that is as warm as the blood in your Body, you must resist!

What does it matter if *I* suffer when he is as truly cold and hard as Marble, insensible to the inroads of weather and the winds that raise dust during the season of Drought. What is the use of going back to room number 15, shut in there before the mirror that reflects back your image, as if it were being mirrored in the still water. No, Signora Adelaide, I have escaped from it all, and the Blood that glided along like a stream must have been like the water of the River T which you know so well, lapping against the resistant Marble Walls, for it is always colder than Blood whatever the surrounding temperature happens to be.

And now I fled on foot away down from Fort C with the intention of taking a train for the place where you, his respected Mother, live, but instead I threw myself exhausted on my bed, and there on the pillow I called on him. I called on Him to witness that I believe in him, Ignazio, as I believe in Saint Anne, and may the Virgin and her Blessèd Son forgive me and Don Vincenzo too, but I believe in him as I believe in the Maker of Heaven and Earth, nor is it too much for me to believe in miracles such as the Resurrection of the Body and the Transfiguration of Ignazio Matteoli into the Bridge.

And I implore you, Respected Mother, to be good

enough to let me know the events that are scheduled to take place in your native Town to which I intend to come and pay my homage during the next holidays that are allotted me. I beg you furthermore, Mother, and your Husband, the Bridge's father, a chemist by profession as I know, to forgive me, for any inaccuracies you both may find in this long story, the kind I have never been accustomed to tell. But for that you must lay the blame, as I have already mentioned, on my inadequate Education in the State Schools.

Luigina, here present also, conveys her respects at this point where I am compelled to stop, exhausted by the great Burden of grief that I have undergone these last days.

Trusting to have the opportunity of presenting my Respects in person before long,

I remain, believe me,
Your Devoted Servant,
Egisto Cartoni.

IV

The night had been stifling and had seemed endless. The chemist sitting in his pyjamas behind the counter had not left his shop; he had been checking his accounts now for many hours, then, having dusted the centre shelf, he began attaching labels to the porcelain jars. Every now and again he glanced at the pendulum clock that hung above the shop-door which he kept exactly synchronized with that of San Rocco. Every quarter you could hear it strike from the campanile on the other side of the river. The silence was broken too by the sound of footsteps; someone was pacing up and down with nervous monotony inside the chemist's flat. At a quarter past six these steps had hastily descended the stairs and you could hear a garden gate creak. Adelaide Matteoli had gone out.

The lights along the embankment had been extinguished; day had begun. The river was low in its bed and gurgled as usual as it lapped against the walls. The dusty plane-trees stretched out their finger-like foliage in all directions. They were huge trees with brown scored trunks. Signora Adelaide walked slowly past them, pausing to support herself against first one and then another of them as she advanced. She was wearing a black costume coat and round the collar she had knotted a lace kerchief.

She stopped at the bridge. Some coloured bunting was stretched across both ends and small white-washed barriers effectively prevented access. The previous day it had been swept out and carefully washed down and it was now gleaming in the early light of dawn. At each extremity of the bridge his name had been carved in the marble – "Ponte Ignazio Matteoli."

The ornamental plants and trees despatched from the capital of the Province had arrived the day before and were aligned along the balustrade – monkey-puzzles, aspidistras, and azaleas. Banners fluttered

amongst them, The parish red-carpet marked the head
of the bridge where the ceremony would be initiated.
The bandstand, however, had been erected at the
farther end of the bridge where the procession would
arrive. The Civic Band had already been rehearsing
the tunes which had been blared forth loudly from
open windows during the August evenings.

Up to five o'clock on the afternoon before, the
Bridge's mother, Adelaide, had still been full of hope.
"It was he who started the workmen off," she had
said to herself, "So the project is *his* – drawings,
measurements, and the site. You will see that Ignazio
will be back here on the day of its inauguration. He
will hear himself acclaimed as he deserves after the
completion of this long task."

But when the workmen pointed out the two tablets
bearing the name of the bridge inscribed on them,
Adelaide had begun to tremble. The Christian and
surname of her son son cut in the surface of the rectangle of white marble as if on a tombstone – Ponte
Ignazio Matteoli – on an arch that extended like a
white sheet across the two banks, sealed with a white
tombstone which to the accompaniment of tolling bells
was being inserted in the wall at both ends. The men
were whistling as they completed the job, but "foreman Egisto" was not present.

"Get back!" shouted the man in charge to the boys
who were invading the bridge now that the barriers
had been removed.

"It's a miracle," said a voice behind Adelaide. "*Our* Ignazio. I remember how as a boy he used to stare into the river as he is doing now."

Adelaide swung round.

"Does it look like him?"

Dr Carletti, the local health officer, stared at her. "You must be proud of him, Signora Adelaide, as indeed we all are."

"Do you think it is like him?"

Adelaide took a step forward and placed her hand on the parapet. It was a cool brow, as cool as on the occasion when she had rescued him from the bath, and white too as then but calm.

"Ignazio," said Adelaide. "Ignazio," she repeated.

The bridge had not stirred; the doctor had gone.

"Dear, dear Ignazio," she murmured. "Can't you hear me?" And she caressed the outstretched body of the bridge which was as smooth as a beardless boy. She passed her hand to and fro, and it soon became as cool as the marble it caressed. Then she leaned over the marble and applied her warm cheek to it; then she kissed the parapet coping again and again with her eyes closed.

It was like kissing a corpse. The same frozen perfection. And yet once again she kissed the motionless stone, smoothed it with both hands, murmured Ignazio's name and continued her kisses in her efforts to breathe a little warmth into the impassive marble.

"Ignazio!"

It was a strange, sudden cry. She shouted again as the stone had begun to quiver under her lips with an almost imperceptible vibration.

"Ignazio!"

She gripped the edge of the parapet with both hands, lunged forward with her whole body. She approached her lips again. No; it was not an illusion. The bridge was responding; it vibrated to her call. More a diffuse tingling perhaps than a vibration, but Adelaide received it with her whole body. With her lips, her womb, her open palms, Adelaide drank absorbed the trembling of her son who lay extended beneath her.

A lorry descending from the *Viale dei Platani* slowed down somewhere behind her; she did not hear it. "It's the new bridge," remarked the driver insistently. "They've finished it at last." The lorry proceeded on its way down the valley.

The bridge had stopped trembling but Adelaide did not leave the parapet where she lay at full length. She could hear the river murmuring beneath her with the same ear as the bridge's. It was a gentle, monotonous gurgle which lulled one to sleep. An occasional chuckle seemed to be intermingled with it, punctuated by the chirrup of the cicadas from the near-by plane-trees. The bridge stood motionless and at the spot where Adelaide was extended had even become warm. With her cheek against the marble she began to murmur Ignazio's name once more.

When two masons invited her to descend she looked at them with a smile and got them to help her down.

One of them said, "You might fall from there. Are you feeling ill?"

"No," Adelaide replied," I can stand all right."

Other workmen moved round her, arranging the flowers and shifting the white-washed barriers which they loaded on to a handcart drawn up where the plane-trees began. On the other bank the bandsmen were taking their places on the stand. In the absence of uniforms they had been issued with black caps with glossy peaks that gleamed throughout the whole ceremony.

The crowd began to press round Adelaide. They were the inhabitants of T, some of whom had arrived one at a time, others in little groups. Andrea, the chemist, had come up alone and was staring at the bridge which reflected back the light. He drew out his watch from his waistcoat pocket at intervals.

"It's the best in the district." The verdict could be heard repeatedly on every side. "But who would have thought it. It was one of our local inhabitants that wanted it. He's given his life for it, there's no doubt about that. After two years. The whole nation knows his story now. They say a book's going to be written and the story will be told to all the school-children in the whole Republic. I remember him as a boy – just after he had had diphtheria."

"Stand back, gentlemen!" cried a voice behind the group.

A crimson carpet divided the crowd as it was unrolled by the Commune messenger and his nephew, a bare-footed lad with chestnut coloured hair. Adelaide found herself in the front rank at one edge of the carpet with Andrea opposite her on the other.

Like a river of blood the carpet invaded the bridge, dyeing its pallor for a stretch of several yards. The bare-foot boy knelt down and swept the blood down with his brush, removing the particles of wet sawdust that marked it. Then, still on his knees and continuing his brushing he withdrew and found his way back onto the macadamized roadway.

By this time the band had struck up a march and the bells of San Rocco were in full peal. Next a procession headed with two banners came into sight on the square of the plane-trees.

In it advanced the Mayor, the Rector, the Prefect, all bare-headed and wearing white gloves. They were followed by students of the University to which Ignazio had belonged. A laurel wreath was borne by two young men; one of them, the paler of the two, was Egisto Cartoni, the Barber of the *Regina Coeli* Prison.

The procession stopped where the red carpet began. Egisto Cartoni and his companion laid the wreath on the stone that bore the name of the bridge. The crowd fell silent and everyone's eyes were on them.

The bridge lay there, binding the two banks closely together; the embankment walls had been strengthened and raised where it had proved necessary. The river with all its violence now seemed far away, said the Mayor in his speech, and henceforward it would be harnessed to work the power stations. No longer would it constitute a threat to the dwelling houses and the town inhabitants; from now on they need anticipate nothing but prosperity from the fury of the waters; within six months the Power station at the south of the Ponte Vecchio would be in use.

The Mayor spoke in low deliberate tones, mentioned the various stages in Ignazio Matteoli's life and also took the opportunity of telling the assembly what power in kilowatts the river would soon be capable of producing. The people of T listened in silence and gazed in turn at the bridge, the river and Mayor Felici's rough features. When he had finished his oration the trumpets at the other bank played a fanfare and the coloured bunting was lowered. For a moment the bridge shone like a mirage under the collective gaze of the onlookers and the Mayor was the first to step on to it, followed by Adelaide, the Prefect, the Rector, Barber Egisto Cartoni, the chemist, and the flags and banners of the University.

Behind them came the inhabitants in silence, all of them bare-headed. The procession stopped in the middle and lined the embankments on either side. The turbid river swirled along the valley between them. The sultry August air shimmered round the band-stand where a march was being played full blast by the musicians as they stood there awaiting the arrival of the procession from the other bank.

It advanced in slow time. It had passed; the ranks were broken. The bridge had been declared open, and the bandsmen continued to play their solemn march.

Adelaide placed a hand on the parapet, smiling at the ovation in a vague kind of way.

"Thank you," she said as she chafed his cold foot – the foot of a little boy who had just come out of his bath.

The chemist paced up and down absorbed in his thoughts. A cluster of boys had gathered up the ribbon which, since it had been cut and the traffic was free to circulate again, lay abandoned on the ground. It was a tricolour ribbon which would make a useful rope for skipping or measuring the length of the bridge.

Swallows were boldly swooping down on the scene, but some, frightened by the music, had retreated under the eaves of the Alms-Houses. A number of the old men had been leaning out of the windows watching them. The officials returned to their places in the cars and there was a slamming of doors. A siren wailed out the midday signal, and the bell ringer tugged on his rope.

The crowd dispersed. The bandsmen, mopping the sweat off their faces, climbed down from the stand. The chemist reopened his shop.

Everyone was talking about the bridge – and future developments.

Ideas were suggested and approved. The proprietor of the *Caffè Centrale* pointed out the newly-arrived allotment of shop furniture to the barman. The electrician had promised to install fluorescent lighting in both his windows. The work-van of the *Società Elettrica Provinciale* was parked in the centre of the square, and within a few days the street-lighting would be completed. The bridge would have its full share. Eight lamps it would have and they would be immediately recognized at night from a great distance away. An arc-lamp too that would be visible even from the Observatory at R situated at the top of the mountain.

Demetrio

I

ONE OF THE LIFT-BOYS had asked for an interview. That was three days ago. The note was marked "urgent". The general manager rang the bell.

"Get me the file about Rosati, please, Demetrio Rosati, and send the boy up."

The secretary went off to carry out his orders. The manager stretched his legs out under his desk and lit a cigar. He puffed away complacently, looking at the clock-face through half-closed eyes. Nicknamed the "Frog" on account of his jerky, irregular gait, his flat features, a nose that was on almost the same plane as his cheeks, he was impolite most of the time and practically always irritable. They said he drank. Be that as it may, his secretary had orders to bring him a pint of cold milk every day at eleven o'clock which he drank systematically but with evident distaste, like someone on a diet.

He lived alone in a room in the Hotel Marini, not more than a few steps away from the department store. When his wife could not stand him any longer, she had gone off to live with a man from Milan, one of the branch managers. The Frog had then sent his only

131

daughter to a boarding school but he visited her less and less as the years went by.

When the Frog made a tour of inspection of the departments, a shudder ran through the male and female assistants lined up behind the counters or along the corridors, all on their best behaviour. Nothing escaped him and, what was more, he noted everything down. He fined and dismissed employees for the most trivial reasons. The price-ticket was not prominent enough on this or that article; goods that had been sold had not been replaced and put on show quickly enough; a shop-girl hadn't her registered number pinned on her overall; one of the girls who had failed to notice his arrival had continued giggling with her companion.

The Frog's eyes would almost leave their sockets.

"He's in a vile temper!" they would murmur.

Without any audible comment the manager noted down his observations in the diary which the board of directors presented to him with unfailing regularity every New Year with their compliments. It was useless to produce an excuse.

He would curl his lips scornfully and point his incredibly long, nicotine-stained forefinger. Then, as usual, he would jerk his way up the red-striped carpet or glide smoothly off on the moving staircase to the floor above, bearing his distended belly on his thin, slightly bowed legs. His secretary knew at once from the memorandum-book he wielded in his hands that

some unfortunate person had received a severe reprimand. It was not surprising that very few of the staff
sought an interview except for serious reasons. No one
was anxious to draw attention to himself.

"I wonder why that little lift-boy wants to let himself in for it," thought the secretary as she held his file
in front of her.

Her boss was still puffing noisily at his cigar. The
spring air came in through the open window accompanied by a chorus of cries from newspaper-sellers.

"Shut the window before you go. I must have some
peace!" He felt exhausted that day, and had it not
been for that wretch of a lift-boy he would have lain
down on the settee. The doctor had warned him against
arteriosclerosis.

Slowly he extracted the sheet from the envelope and
read. "Demetrio Rosati, son of the late Federico and
Isabella Crespi, resident in the via delle Acacie, Block
28, Staircase L, Tenant number 30. Period of service:
2 years. General report 'Good'. Fines: None.

"It's preposterous," he muttered.

What did the boy want? A step up perhaps; promotion to the cleaning department? How old was he?
Sixteen.

"Too young for that yet."

He rang, and the boy was at the door almost at once.
He was small all right. You wouldn't have thought he
was even fourteen. His red tunic with its brass buttons
and the braid down the trouser-legs made him look like

one of the boys that distribute bills about travelling circuses at cinema entrances.

"Sit down."

The boy did so and laid his red hat with its gold-braided peak on his knees. He was pale and he stared at the floor. The manager scrutinized him. He was enjoying the boy's embarrassment. He had asked for the interview so *he* should break the ice. But the boy continued silent, his eyes fixed on the polished floor.

"Well?"

"Well, sir . . ."

He swallowed. He swallowed again. The Frog sank in his seat behind the desk, planted his elbows on the plate-glass surface and cupped his chin. He had stopped puffing at his cigar. It lay in the ash-tray, and the smoke rose up from it in a slow, continuous spiral between them. The wind must have got up outside because a ripple ran through the curtain and struck against the glass-panes.

The Frog's eyes stared relentlessly from under his pink eyelids and above the bluish pouches underneath. Demetrio now lifted his gaze, and a gush of warm blood rose to his cheeks. He managed to stammer, "I've come to give my notice."

In his effort to say something he was unconsciously fidgeting with his hat and bending back the peak.

"Look after your hat. It is still the property of the firm which employs you."

Demetrio swallowed again.

"Go on," said the Frog.

"That's all, Sir."

And Demetrio stood up. He wanted to go to the door.

"That's all. It was just to say that," he repeated.

"Sit down."

The cigar smoke quivered between them and, caught in a draught of air, began to swirl round. A motor-horn gave a peremptory warning note on the piazza below.

"Sit down," he commanded again.

Demetrio obeyed.

Why on earth had the boy come in person, the Frog kept asking himself. A letter would have sufficed, a mere card with a few relevant words. Leaving a department store wasn't such a complicated business as getting a job in one for which you were required to produce school-leaving certificates and all kinds of references. It was easy enough to give your notice; no one ever presented himself in person to the staff manager for that. It was his secretary's job to hand the leaver his employment book and insurance card fully stamped. In all these years the manager had never even said good-bye to department heads when they resigned or left to retire or when they were sacked for unsatisfactory salesmanship, abuse of authority or general inefficiency. That a lift-boy should come and tender his resignation in person was just fantastic. . . .

The Frog gave a start and laughed. He pressed his finger on the lowest bell-push.

"Please hand me the list of applicants for the lift

post," he said to his secretary. "This young gentleman is leaving our service. Apparently the air of the shop doesn't suit him."

And he gave her a wink as he bounced on his revolving armchair.

The young lady reappeared with the list almost immediately.

"Come over here, boy."

Demetrio obeyed.

"Look!"

It was a list of names drawn up in alphabetical order like a class-register.

"The claimants to your throne, *your* throne," he went on. "Eight hundred and twenty-four applications in four months. But that means nothing to you, young idiot. Yet they give you a good report, and you don't seem to have any special counter-attraction at home. When you go it'll merely be a matter of whom to choose next. I can have them dark or fair, Venetians or Sicilians. But let's get this point clear. There's no problem as far as I'm concerned. All that matters is that your successor should have the same measurements – neck-band, shoulders and leg-length. The uniform is, I see, in a good condition. The cloth isn't shiny yet and the shoes only need a new sole. Don't think I'm trying to keep you, Demetrio, I've neither the right nor the wish to do so; so don't worry on that score. It's the call of freedom, it seems. The air of the store doesn't suit you or perhaps the lift cables squeak too much . . ."

And the Frog laughed again, shaking all over. A ray of sunlight fell on his head, and his bald pate shone like a mirror. Two tears appeared in his eyes and he quickly wiped them away with the back of his hand.

Demetrio stood there with his head bent forward. He had been reading some of the names: Angeletti, Angelini, Angelucci, Badiali, Biondi. Slowly he stretched his arm across the desk and handed the list back.

"But even they one day . . ."

"To hell with them!"

The Frog jerked himself up out of the chair arms which had held him prisoner up till then and stood beside him, tall, erect, threatening.

"And you the last-comer!"

Demetrio could feel his breath on his face, and between his tobacco-stained teeth he saw the empty box inside furnished with soft, whitish gums. He stood his ground. The manager panted in impotent fury and leaned against his desk.

"The last-comer officially announces his departure. We order military honours for him. The department store shall be decorated with tricolour notices. Farewell, Demetrio! The lift-brat is called to higher duties and abandons his post. The whole staff, the manager at the head, salute in him the pioneer of liberty!

"A little whipper-snapper, that's all you are. The milk hardly dry on your lips and now you want to paddle your own canoe. During the thirty-four years of my service here I alone have controlled the fate of lift-boys, deciding who to sack, who to promote to be shop-assistants and so on, right up to heads of departments and even inspectors. I have assigned the jobs to generations over five floors – mothers, daughters, cashiers, cleaners. And not one has ever ventured to give notice. Not one! In the palm of my hand I hold grandfathers in the packing-room and messenger and porter nephews. Each one of them is bound up with somebody else and they all take orders from me, every one of them. But just you alone . . ."

The secretary walked across the room carrying the bottle of milk. There was a faint clink as the beaker made contact with the glass surface. The liquid was poured out. It gurgled through the narrow neck, invaded the cone-shaped space, filled it to the brim. The secretary gave the impression of intentionally delaying the arrangement of the tray between the arms of the chair. She now placed it carefully in the middle. She shook out the ash-tray and passed a duster over it which she had produced from her overall pocket. She seemed for a moment to be anxious to stop and watch the boy. She gave him a rapid but interested glance. He was pale again: his obstinately lowered eyes were levelled at the edge of the desk.

The Frog took advantage of this interruption to regain his breath. At the appearance of Signorina Luisa he had stopped talking and his breathing became normal again. He began to stride up and down behind the boy and continued his gesticulations.

When Signorina Luisa had restored the ash-tray to its position on the table, she inquired whether the *signor direttore* wanted the milk brought over to him. The Frog stopped at the sound of her voice and stared at her but it was evident that he had not taken in what she said. His eyes, strangely glassy, were fixed in a stare and even his eyelids did not flicker.

The secretary repeated her question.

"Get out. Get out quickly," he growled.

"A rebel that's what he is," he went on.

He had slumped down between the arms of his office chair. He was talking quietly, as if to himself.

"And before very long, your companion, the operator of number 2 lift, will be requesting an audience with the manager, wanting to follow you in your path to freedom. You who were barefoot when you first arrived, couldn't even talk properly and didn't know when to remove your cap. And in two years, look what we've made of you! Polite, meticulous in the wearing of a uniform, *our* uniform which is respected in every quarter of the town and in all our other branches, a uniform more highly esteemed even than a coat-of-arms or an 'order', a uniform that hundreds of boys would give their eyes for, quite apart from the pleasure they get from showing themselves off in it. . . . But this fellow is going to take it off, lay it aside in exchange for the self-sufficient clothes that he came in."

He spoke hurriedly and in a whisper.

Demetrio appeared not to be listening. He continued

to stare at the lower edge of the desk and run his eyes rapidly from there to the edge of the carpet where a rhombus-pattern started. His face was paler than ever; his lips were tightly pressed over his teeth. He held his red hat upside down behind his back between his thumb and forefinger, and on its white rayon lining, just above the faint ring caused by perspiration, the store trade-mark stood out in black.

He did not look at the manager who had turned his back on him. The latter was talking as if for himself alone, tumbling down the scale in an interminable soliloquy.

"They map out a meteoric career for themselves, full of eagerness to get on. At sixteen they give in their notice, all agog to seek their fortune and consort with toughs and wide boys in the various dives on the town outskirts. They want to work on their own – that's what they tell you – but they haven't got a half-penny in their pockets, no kind of guarantee behind them, no, not even the name of a respectable firm which can exert enough daily pressure on them to force them to behave. Then they begin to drift. Puffed up with self-importance at the age of sixteen. Plain selfish, that's what they are. Boys who have led completely sheltered lives up to the present. . . ."

He would have gone on and on in this vein, but just then the boy turned round and made his presence felt. A hot flush had mounted to his cheeks again. He leaned forward and looked like one of those cherubs

carved on church roofs who keep a watchful eye on the
congregation from their position of vantage on the beams.

His hat had slipped from his hand while he had been
screwing it up, and now it lay at his feet in an amor-
phous heap. At last his teeth released their grip and his
lips opened.

"You're wrong, Sir. It is true that I am leaving the
lift-service, but yet . . . you see . . . No . . . Look. I
didn't want . . ."

He stamped his foot to emphasize the point he was
trying to make and paused for breath.

The Frog, still silent, fell back on to the leather seat
of his office chair and the boy continued to stare down
at him. All at once out came a spate of simple, well-
chosen words.

He had been trying to get this interview for the last
three days so that he could request the *signor direttore*
to release him from his service . . . that is to say,
immediately. Immediately, he repeated. Within a
week. That was why he had presented himself in
person. He realized that this business might drag on
for a month otherwise, with his papers going from one
desk to the other, waiting to be signed and stamped.

He shook his head, and with the palm of his hand
brushed back the hair which hung over his eyes in
clusters of curls.

For three days they had kept him in suspense, he
said. He had been going up and down, shouting his
patter in front of the lift gates. What he had really

been wanting to do was to come up here to the manage-
ment where he now had the honour to find himself,
so that he could ask the manager himself to release him.
He would hand over the uniform; he was ready to
remove it at once. He was glad to hear that the manage-
ment would soon find a young lad to replace him.
A wistful, sympathetic light came into his eyes. He
thought of his successor and was silent.

The Frog rose from the soft chair-springs with an
effort as if he was extracting himself from a marsh.
The small boy drew back and collected his cap.

Luisa appeared in the doorway. She was coming to
remove the tray. But the milk was still up to the brim
of the glass beaker. Surprised, she looked over at the
manager who was half-standing up, livid. The boy on
the other hand seemed at ease, and Luisa thought it
wisest not to interfere.

As soon as he had pulled himself upright, the Frog
strode unsteadily on his bow legs over to the window.
He felt as if he was choking. Slowly he opened the
window and as he did, voices rose up all round him
and seemed to enclose him. Motor horns mingled with
the cries of the newspaper-sellers, while away in the
distance a mason sang from the roof he was repairing
as he struck rhythmically at a stone.

He moved to the edge of the balcony.

The boy remained where he was near the desk. He
had dropped his head again, and his hands in which he
was nervously twisting his hat, had begun to tremble.

Why didn't they let him go at once?

"These boys," muttered the Frog.

He closed the window again and returned to his desk. Slowly he sipped his milk.

"Well?"

He took his time.

He pressed the bell-push and ordered his secretary to clear the table.

Signorina Luisa did so.

She had left the door ajar, and now from the depths of the shop came the usual rush-hour din. It was a confused noise, quite unlike that which rose up from the street – a shrill lisping of, mostly, female voices came up the shaft. It was the voice of power.

The purr of the lifts seemed to merge with the voices. The beehive was buzzing peacefully and securely. At intervals the sound became more distant and turned into a gentle rustle of leaves, only to change into the storms of the holiday rushes when the department heads like helmsmen showered their cries over the seething tides, calling out frantic orders at every moment. The lift gates slammed with more violence than ever, and the lift-boys cries of "going down", "going up!" rose in accelerated tempo, half-speed, then full-speed as the customers were loaded and unloaded without pause.

The manager would sally forth at such times to inspect the various departments. And how satisfying he found it! The staff, undaunted, was resisting every onslaught. And what a sight! Some on the port side, others lowering sail and bearing down on the jewellery, handbags and glove departments; others again were plunging about among "outfits for youths" or shirts that had been spread out on the sale-counters. Shirts in every size and material, silk, rayon or cotton. His eyes dwelt lovingly on the sale-cards which he himself had composed for the occasion. "Competitive prices"; "Exceptional offer", "Please do not touch"; "Everything for the table". He watched the queue with pride as it paused in front of the notices on which the organization of the departments was explained in detail. And his contented heart beat triumphantly and with satisfaction – why not? – before the counters where goods already purchased and waiting to be wrapped were gradually rising in great piles. And there they were on the open shelves for everyone to see – tricycles with red handle-bars, refrigerators, ladies pure cambric hankies, orderly bundles of bed and table linen.

It was the great testing time for the apprentices, shop-girls, and porters. Some of the girls did in fact succumb.

Ready as he always was to lend first-aid to any customer that fainted, it happened sometimes that he had to cope with some of the shop-girls themselves in a similar plight while they were serving, on the gift, toy or sweet counter. Such an incident, for they usually fainted in the rush period, far from being an interruption only increased the general air of bustle and gave a special flavour to the crush and struggle in front of the counters. So the manager was careful not to dismiss assistants who suffered from such temporary indispositions; on the contrary he fostered them. And if, after closing-time a head of department proposed to transfer the unfortunate girl to another counter, he reinstated her where she had fainted – the toys, gifts, tobacco or sweet counter as the case might be.

After these memorable days, how sweetly evening seemed to descend in the vast island of the store, when the grilles were closed, lights extinguished and only a few dim side-lamps remained to indicate the field of battle. And the departments were overcome with a sudden silence; every floor from the top to the base- ment. And the lifts were grounded to have a rest and the moving stairway had ceased to move and you could walk down it like any other staircase. And the staff discarded their uniforms. And each girl-assistant swiftly slipped out of the exit door.

The goods, in the special covers which protected them from the dust, also rested in peace – the unsold wares that still remained. There were cups and beakers with their throats empty, trumpets in search of breath, brightly-coloured books with their pages uncut, women's corsets, cold and empty without their occu- pants, umbrellas enclosed in black sheaths, ties of every kind, bright, variegated, sombre.

Alone, leaning on the narrow hand-rail, the Frog descended the escalator, while tailor's dummies, some in evening dress, some with floral-patterned fronts of some plastic material and bow-ties, flew past him, withdrawing respectfully into the shadow of their corners where they were safe from collisions.

Perhaps it was this hour of defeat, which he had to experience in the evenings of rush periods when his services were required after closing-time, that the small lift-boy hated so much.

The manager raised his head. He must ask him.

Meanwhile Demetrio was awaiting his marching orders.

A small boy who, stripped of his braided uniform, wasn't worth a half-penny; look at him there with those pallid cheeks that hadn't yet lost their bloom.

"Immediately," he had said.

"Well," repeated the Frog. He gripped his cigar, relit it and began to puff out smoke.

"I understand you," he said. "You want to leave the place and if I am detaining you now it is certainly not with any idea of trying to make you change your mind. I just want you to realize what you are doing. Then I wash my hands of it all. What amazes me is that you should be in such a hurry to leave. There's still one question I would like to ask you. . . ."

The boy raised his head.

"Well?"

They looked at each other for some time in a strangely detached way. Then all at once the Frog spoke and asked the boy the name of the firm in the town which — since his triumph over the store — he proposed to honour with his presence.

Was that all he wanted to ask him?

Now that the door of suspicion was closed in his mind, the boy smiled. He did not yet know anything very definite but he had already applied for a job with a cabinet-maker. He was expecting a reply hourly; meantime he was going to lend his brother a hand.

It was the Frog's turn to laugh. His face a greenish tinge under his glasses, he smiled as he emitted cigar smoke from his nostrils. His head was sunk into his shoulders. The boy, still blushing, continued his meandering story. He gave the impression of following some kind of graphic pattern with his eyes, an odd, complicated pattern that would have been difficult to read even if it had been inscribed on a white wall. And without his explanations, no one could have unravelled its mysteries as Demetrio seemed able to in a voice, now breaking with emotion, now as firm and decisive as a cutting edge.

Inexperienced and frail as he was, with almost girlish limbs, Demetrio had launched out boldly into his adventure. Indeed the objective which appeared before his eyes like a mirage would have made anybody's mouth water and especially the Frog's at that moment. It was a post for which it would be reasonable to exchange not only the control of a lift but the control of the whole system of bell-pushes where all you had to

do was press your finger and people of every age of
both sexes presented themselves in scores from every
department, offering their services.

It was for a post of this kind – yes, immortality it
was – that Demetrio was leaving the store. The pattern
unfolded itself without interruption, without a hiatus,
flawless. Perfect. Logical. It had been Antonio who
had first seen it all so clearly. Antonio, his elder
brother.

What could the Frog know about him.

"Antonio," he murmured.

And who on earth was this Antonio?

II

"He leaves his traces everywhere!"

Silent, pervasive, unruffled. Like oil when it is
poured out and spreads everywhere, penetrating each
crack, flowing into every interstice, filling every space
and settling smoothly on the surface.

"He spreads like oil," his sisters would say, referring
to their elder brother.

Signs of his work were all round them. Bits of steel
wire, rope, insulating tape, empty spools and coils,
pliers, stoppers lay about everywhere – on chests-of-
drawers, on the beds, by the wash-tub, on the kitchen-
stove, in the sink. Heaps of wood-shavings, tins and
cardboard boxes, piles of straw lay scattered around or
assembled on a tray. There were cuttle-fish bones of

every size like those that the receding tide leaves behind on the seaweed. There were conch shells, fragments of bamboo-shoot, pumpkin gourds – beachcombings after the high autumn tides or objects found outside the town limits or by some garden. Mostly, however, they had been salvaged from the river.

The river provided an unending supply from which Antonio obtained his raw material. It constituted his real mine, always open, ready and inexhaustible.

He went off alone to search its depths. With infinite skill and patience he prodded the surface of the water with a kind of trident and succeeded in extracting all sorts of flotsam. He caught the various objects as they floated by rapidly with the current. In a series of deft movements he would line them up on the level shore – corks, iron frames, chair-bottoms. Sometimes he even landed the whole shaft of a hand-cart intact or a shutter-board that the river in full spate had wrenched off some warehouse, accompanied maybe with a broken fragment of doll or the leg of a rocking-horse.

Patiently, alone under the spell of a hot afternoon sun or under a gentle shower of rain, Antonio would wade out to rescue these treasures from the water.

Some of the objects had drifted there from a considerable distance; others had been thrown in quite recently, as he could see from their perfect state of preservation or by the label which had not yet been washed off.

Antonio would subject each article or fragment to a

close scrutiny, turn it over in his hand, test the density or resistance of this or that material with his teeth, measure the length of pieces of stick or the thickness of a plank, toy with the torso of a wooden doll, meditating in silence on the use to which he would put it and whether it was worth taking away or not. And if it wasn't, back went the doll or the plank into the river-bed and he would try another throw with his harpoon.

Holding on to a bush, he leant out from the shore but often an apparently important piece of wood failed to "bite" or having "bitten" would jerk itself away and slide off on the current. He lunged at it, infuriated, hanging over the surface in a supreme effort. But the relic on the dark surface which was beyond his reach bobbed quietly away as in a dream.

Then Antonio, annoyed, would draw back but continue to stare covetously at the object which drifted off towards its own dissolution.

"I must find a new type of instrument," he murmured as he twirled the trident in his hands or cleared his net of rubbish. The table that had evaded capture and the seat seemed to have come from some boat – well-planed down, with well-turned corners and duly seasoned – they would have been just the thing for him, or rather for Angioletto, the owner of the cycle-shop who had been plaguing him for a bench this last month.

Antonio's particular skill lay in fact in his ability to

assess at once the potentialities of these often shapeless relics in relation to his neighbours' needs. Whether it was a work-bench for the owner of the cycle shop or a plank for covering the old shop-keeper's dog-kennel.

After a few hours' work everything took on a new form in his hands. When the neighbours saw him appear at the corner of the square with his load, they said, "Here comes the workshop."

He walked quickly, as was his custom, maintaining the pace of the person who is obliged to cover considerable distances. And since he lived on the edge of the town, on the occasions when he was unsuccessful in riding on the buffers of the tram, he had to trust to his own legs to go down to the town centre and pay a visit to the big store.

Entrance was free, and it was thus that he familiarized himself with the latest novelties and in the most varied fields of knowledge – electricity, hydraulics, household articles, shooting and fishing.

The dusted objects shone on the shelves. They had no crack, scratch or blemish. He sometimes felt an impulse to stroke them but the assistants kept an eye on him whenever he began to linger in front of a splendid electric drill or the latest model of gun for under-water fishing. Lovingly he would feast his eyes on them.

The world was not solely composed of fragments that had to be stuck together with tar or carpenters' glue, though you might be inclined to think so if you lived where Antonio lived, among mended curtains, chairs with the springs resting on the floor, rickety tables, drawers which, instead of sliding smoothly, creaked as they were pushed back because of the damp.

Here, on the other hand, a department-head was showing a young married couple a cupboard for bed-linen with twenty-eight drawers which hardly emitted a sigh as they were pulled out, and a touch of one finger sufficed to push back. All this made Antonio's mouth water; for him it was like a miracle. So, too, was the sight of this electric geyser fixed to the wall, rotund and self-important above the floral-patterned porcelain bath, displaying its trade-name on its maternally warm belly.

Yet even on the grey shelves of the store, the various articles seemed to float as on the leaden surface of the river. They were motionless, but he had no fish-hook to yank them out with. He could inspect them from above and below, try them out, ask how they worked, and, if the shop-girl would be good enough to demonstrate: here was the latest model of sewing-machine, completely silent, capable, if the description was to be believed, of tacking miles and miles of cloth in twenty-four hours. And beside it was a vacuum-cleaner that consumed dust and could dislodge it from the most unlikely places from mattresses to statues of saints. It shone there, perfect, brand-new and shiny, specially made for swallowing those almost invisible specks of dust which almost immediately find their way back to the surface of the object that has been treated. A small, grey, shapeless oblong bag was the insatiable stomach into which the bits of rubbish were sucked. A slight tap, a regurgitation and the stomach was emptied of its contents into the bucket and then began to contract and quiver again with renewed appetite.

Antonio stared hard at it, his mouth open in his concentrated effort. Gliding between one counter and the next he gazed in admiration. There were electric washing-machines, the sort in which the soap suds were churned round for hours unaided by human hand and driers which were made to avoid hanging-out the washing and brought the warm south winds indoors in the depths of winter. Then there were silent and rapid typewriters like millipedes and mixers that make a paste as smooth as spun sugar, with all their quivering organs enclosed and well protected in the framework of the machine; and fire-proof electric stoves, insulated resistance coils; hairdressers' permanent-wave machines and electric hair-driers – helmets lined up like soldiers on parade, one already wearing the red stripe of promotion, another chromium-plated and resplendent, a third, transparent like a jelly-fish.

They are all up there on the shelves, objects made of plastic and toughened aluminium, beech or chestnut or marble, priced and at anchor. All you have to do is remove the little ticket and the object would be in your hands, parcelled up and tied with an elaborate bow.

"There's some writing with it," murmured Antonio and bent forward to decipher the staggering figure. He let them give him a copy of "instructions for use" to digest at his leisure. And at home he studied them. With a pencil he sketched the various sections, armatures, pulleys, and springs on the marble top of the kitchen table.

Then he would show Demetrio how it worked.

"Look."

Demetrio stood attentive and silent behind him. He saw how it was all connected up section by section, coils fitted on rings, triangles broken up into rectangles; arrows carrying piston-rods, pistons rising and falling, the positive and negative poles fixed near the coils revolving on their own power.

Demetrio watched, fascinated. The sponge had already erased those diagrams from the marble top and others, extracted from the pamphlet which Antonio held in his hands made their appearance as he doggedly followed the thread of the explanations, leaping through the alphabet from A to Z in his effort not to get lost in the labyrinth of connecting leads and terminals.

"Look."

This was how Demetrio had learned to know about these things in Antonio's spell-binding words and now he could stare at them in the flesh as they were taken out of the window – objects that normally lay rigid under the spotlight, objects that dispersed or assembled were enclosed within the mystery of the pamphlets that Antonio doted on and which were incomplete without his explanations – dead, with all their organs locked in the secrecy of their own bosom.

"Look."

Antonio had initiated him in all the wonders of the store, and it was Antonio who had persuaded him to apply for a job as a lift-boy.

They had tried the red uniform on him, they had tried the timbre of his voice as he shouted "Going down" or "Third floor". They had taught him the art of managing the controls so that he could pull up smoothly at the various floors. Look, there he was flying up!

III

Demetrio's early days in the store were happy enough.

"Going up," he called out.

He stood stiffly against the open grille-gate of the lift, inviting the customers in. He made an effort not to slam the gate, according to his instructions, and once inside with the passengers he would reel off the various departments in a high-pitched voice.

"Mensunderwearhosieryhaberdasherylace-ware perfumesjewelleryhandbagsbooksconfectionery . . ."

He would unload and dart out at the first floor, hop back and proceed with further announcements during the journey between the floors.

"Draperysoft-furnishinglinenladiessuitsandcoats corsets-aprons."

He recited it all in one rapid breath in his effort to get it out before reaching the third floor and the fourth and so on. He never forgot an item or a department, and he even found time between the floors to listen to passengers' requests on their way up and down.

"Going down."

He was often alone in the lift, and the mirrors reflected back his image. Suspended in the void, he did all the departments in reverse. Then he would take in a new batch of passengers and start the litany again.

Close at hand, now in step with his lift, now out of step, the lift number 2 rose or fell in its shaft. Both quite silent, indefatigable in their journeys, rapid in their loading or unloading, whether they went up or down. The two diminutive experts who stood by the controls rivalled each other in slightness of build; both of them kept the levers, brasswork, and mirrors brightly polished so that they shone in the permanent, opalescent strip-lighting.

"Demetrio has become a lift-boy," Antonio repeated. "Some go for cars or motor-bikes. He's got a lift! And you should see him driving it."

He took Assunta to see for herself.

Once more Demetrio was standing by the open lift-gate. It was the quiet interval in the store, just after they had closed down for lunch. The February sales were on. Multi-coloured remnants had invaded the

ground floor, marked down at clearance prices – or so
it was claimed – ready for the sales-battle. Lengths of
silk, rayon, linen hung from the rails on the first floor,
rigid in the frosty air. They looked like a flotilla of
caravels caught in full sail by the sirocco in midwinter
or sheltering from a south-west gale or mistral. The
general tranquillity was disturbed only by a regular
purring sound that issued from the escalator as it rose
empty between the floors.

Assunta had just left her door followed by Antonio.
She had paused to look round. The automatic gates
sighed more and more plaintively as they closed behind
them. Scattered here and there shop-girls bobbed up and
a white-faced cashier entered the cash-desk and unrolled
a bundle of pink banknotes. A sailor could be seen behind the walnut rail that bordered the escalator. He
glided smoothly upwards, staring straight in front of
him, his hand resting on the rail.

"Come along now," said Antonio, taking his young
sister by the arm.

It was all familiar to him, but it was Assunta's first
visit. She raised her eyebrows and blinked in wonder-
ment. She hesitated like a colt finding its passage
barred by a lorry in a country lane. Its eyes flash, its
neck stiffens; its limbs tremble, yet planted firmly on
the ground they resist the blows, shoves and urgings
of its peasant driver. It remains obdurate. It is still
only a colt with its abundant black mane and though
panic-stricken, its courage never gives out. By now

the lorry driver has switched off his engine and sits laughing with his elbows resting on the steering wheel. He waits patiently. The obstinate creature will have to get over this sort of thing and fall back into the easy gait of its meadow days. In point of fact it is the sound of a whinnying in a field on the other side of the hedge, quite close to the animal, that does the trick, and it starts forward reassured.

Assunta had suddenly discovered Demetrio, near the lift.

"She glided up behind me like a snake," said Demetrio. "'Going up,' I shouted, and up we went. Then I took the lift down and up again several times more with Assunta on board and then we took Antonio as well. Then I let them both out. Finally I had no more passengers and I went up and down by myself."

It had been like a ball bouncing up and down or a shy young falcon that swoops straight down onto its prey and rises without having caught it, tries again, rises, still nervous, swoops and seizes it and then repeats the whole process.

It went on like that the whole day. And even after the shop was shut, Demetrio continued to work his lift. He took in assistants, packers, department-managers, and porters indiscriminately. The goods were already covered over with dust sheets, the lights were out but Demetrio still continued his journeys, even descending into the basement.

And he was also the last to leave. The lift squeaked

and the strip-lighting in the cage shifted in a ghostly
fashion. He seemed to hear the silence breathing in the
pauses every time the gate drew up at one of the floor
levels. Corridors stretched out on all sides. The strip of
red carpet guided Demetrio's steps between the various
counters. He lifted the corner of one of the dust-
sheets and peeped. They were objects with chrom-
ium plated or enamel bodies, porcelain burners and
aluminium feet and were backed with felt.

He switched on the torch which the night-watchman
had passed on to him. The beam shone, probing the
darkness. The kettle seemed to leap up in front of the
tea-cup, the plates squatted, wedged into each other,
regular and round. Shells, sharing the same destiny,
the plates rose up in piles — half a dozen, a dozen, two
dozen; some red, some white or with floral or abstract
designs on them, made of earthenware or china as the
case might be. Some were elegant with a chaste border;
some were of the deep, heavy kind of ware. They
clinked in chorus if you moved them.

His lamp flashed unsteadily from a rocking-horse to a
rubber cushion, from a garden-rake to an oval bedside
mat. The beam of light followed lengths of cotton that
gave off a strange odour of dressing and starch
mingling with that of the linoleum. Rolls of the latter
in many assorted patterns lay about the floor between
the flour-mixers with their huge paunches and the wax
tailor's dummies of boys dressed in sailor-suits with
brown school-satchels slung across their bodies.

"Demetrio!"

He gave a start. The shout came from the watchman on duty beginning on his rounds.

"It's late."

"I'm just off."

He bestrode his bicycle and pedalled off down the main street helped by a following wind. The houses divided as he dashed along the furrow between them. He was hungry. The backs and palms of his hands were covered with a layer of cold. He clapped them together. He leaned on his handle-bars and pressed hard on the pedals. He managed to avoid a couple of sleepy dogs which were lying between the tramlines. The whip of a cabby driving his horse back to the stable cracked within inches of his face. He whistled a greeting and flew past him. Now meadows extended along both sides of the road. A goods train staggered along the sky-line and clamoured under the stars in a kind of drawn-out wail for freedom or at any rate for a quiet siding. A dog's bark rose in the darkness and the smoke of a locomotive descended like a pall where it had stopped outside the station.

A few more turns of his pedals and he was back in his suburb. Slowing down, he swung round a couple of corners and dismounted. With his bicycle slung on his shoulders he went along the passage and across the yard. He paused at the bottom of the staircase.

It happened one strange evening that a voice reached him from above. Demetrio approached the banister and looked up. They were laughing their heads off.

He began to hurry upstairs. It was a wild laugh. A convulsive laugh that descended in a series of croaks, rending the silence of the staircase well.

He went over to the banister again and looked. But the light was too feeble. He began mounting nervously, and when he was on the third-floor landing, he saw him.

"Antonio!"

His arms spread apart, his head thrown back he stood stiffly against the wall, and in the darkness his form stood out against the white-washed wall, a shuddering fresco shaken from head to foot by this strange laughter.

"Antonio!"

He was bent double, pressing his hands against his belly, shrieking with laughter. He drew himself up again and threw his shoulders back and folded his arms. He gave the impression of supporting the wall rather than leaning against it as he stood there overcome by a gust of laughter which shook him mercilessly, not even allowing him to get his breath. He gasped and gave a kind of hysterical guffaw.

"Antonio!"

But he did not hear. He stood alone on the landing. He seemed lost in the despair of ecstasy, far away from them all. But now he had seen and was pointing his finger at Demetrio's back.

T.S.—L

Demetrio turned round but all he could see was the closed door of someone's rooms.

"Antonio!" he repeated. "For God's sake say something. You're frightening me." He went up to him.

But Antonio could not stop laughing and merely moved off. He wanted the younger boy to let him have his laugh out; he wanted to go on laughing like this for ever at the top of his voice, alone as he stood on the brink of the yawning abyss of the victory which was within his grasp and had stimulated this uncontrollable laughter.

So instead of recounting his story, instead of bursting into song or a shout, he just laughed. And the prodigious noise came through his narrow nostrils like a violent and primitive braying.

Demetrio gave a shudder, went up to his brother, embraced him, pressed against him, almost twining his body round him to smother his laughter.

"Can I lend you a hand, Demetrio?"

Carmine had opened the door noiselessly.

They stood locked in each other's arms, quiet, breathing heavily. A beam of light fell right across them.

"No."

"No."

They released their hold. They had calmed down again. The laughter and panting were over. A motor-cycle roared in the courtyard below.

"Good night."

Demetrio collected his bicycle and began to climb up again. Antonio followed him, bent, pensive, his head lowered.

IV

"Demetrio!"

"Yes?"

"What are you doing?"

"Trying to sleep."

"Sleep?"

"Yes."

Demetrio turned towards the wall. Antonio kept rolling over and over in bed. The iron legs of the bedstead creaked and his body shivered between the sheets. The creaking was like that made by the branch of a tree jerked against the railings outside by the wind.

"Demetrio."

"What do you want?"

"Why aren't you asleep?"

"I am!"

"Yes?"

"Good night then!"

Another goods train wailed as it reached the points. Meantime the steady tick of the clock burst relentlessly out of the darkness.

"Demetrio!"

"Yes?"

"Not asleep yet?"

"No."

"Can I switch the light on?"

"Yes."

Antonio switched it on.

Demetrio was already sitting up in bed, his knees pulled up and the yellow counterpane drawn round his chin. He was rather pale, the rims of his eyes were inflamed and at intervals he was shaken by a faint shudder.

Antonio sat up too.

"What a night," he said.

The clock ticked away solemnly in the silence.

"What time is it?"

"Half-past two."

"The express is late tonight."

"Yes it is."

"Are you cold?"

"No."

"I'm suffocating." He leaped out of bed.

"What are you doing?"

There was a break in Demetrio's voice.

"Nothing. Just walking about."

"I say."

"What's up?"

"Antonio, please don't laugh."

"Not laugh?"

"Not like you did before on the stairs. Please don't laugh. I don't want you to. It frightens me."

He had thrown his overcoat over his shoulders and walked to and fro. He looked excited and at intervals let out deep sighs.

"Demetrio."

"Yes."

"Did you notice Assunta?"

"What about her?"

"She's remodelled her style of dress."

"Yes, I noticed."

"And green gloves. I saw her putting stitches on her needles three days ago and they're already drooping from them like vine tendrils. She's been singing as she put them on."

Assunta had been singing. She lay back on the settee, shaping the fingers and singing softly to herself, completely absorbed.

"What did she sing?"

"All sorts of things. Popular songs. The sound rose and fell in the courtyard."

"Yes."

Antonio walked over to the window. The courtyard sank below him quiet and dead within the whitewashed walls. A cold, solemn moon lit up a whole corner. The clothes that hung from the balcony moved gently in the breeze.

"Here comes the express."

It whistled by.

"Twenty minutes late."

"Eighteen."

"It will catch them up."

"Yes."

"At the points."

"Yes."

He turned away from the window and began to walk about again. Demetrio followed him with his eyes.

"Demetrio!"

"Quiet, you'll wake them up!"

"Yes, but I must talk to you."

"Fire away then."

"Make room."

"Come over here."

He leaped on to the other's bed.

"It would be best to put the light out."

The moon came out. It seemed tired and remote but it managed to reach them, bisecting their bed. Antonio was in the beam of light at the foot of the bed. Now that he was enfolded in silence and the bright shaft of light which bathed Demetrio's bed, he felt he could unburden himself.

"It will shine for another hour yet," he said. "It's setting but it is still nearly full. If they hadn't built the balcony opposite we should have it in the room a little longer."

He leaned his neck against the iron bedstead and smiled up at the moon.

"How calm it is," he said. "But I'd like to be by the river. I've only fished once by full-moon and that was during the August holiday when there was hardly any current. The frogs were setting up a deafening croak all round. I had a bathe at dawn."

He spoke with slow deliberation. It was obvious that he was trying to steer round some obstacle, pausing as he slid off into some side-stream of memory.

"The night was sultry, and when I dived into the water the lights on the bridge had only just been put out. I was completely alone, and I swam for nearly half-a-mile."

He fell silent. It was evident that once more he was drifting off with the stream, and Demetrio lay motionless waiting for him to regain the shore while the moon continued to shine down on him peacefully. His shadow extended on the floor beside him, gentle, watchful. When Antonio raised his hands, gesticulating, the shadow assumed the shape of a dog's ears when it pricks them up. Then they drooped again.

"The river has been my chief source of supply and inspiration for years. It's my farm where I reap without sowing. Things spring up according to the seasons. A couple of days ago for example I caught a lamb. There must be a large flock of them in the hills, but I can't understand how the river managed to get hold of them. Perhaps they go down to drink. The first victim can only have been about a week old and had fallen in quite recently. It found its way into my net almost as if it had been looking for a refuge and when I handled it, it seemed to be looking at me. I even shook it in the hope of hearing it bleat."

He repeated the movement now and the ears in the shadow quivered several times in succession.

"I fished two of them out of the river but I put them back bleached so white that when they reach the sea they will already look like foam. But if they keep on getting into the river, I shall see about taking a walk upstream on Sunday. Would you like to come, Demetrio?"

"Yes, I'd like to."

"I'll ask Carmine if I can borrow his bicycle."

"Yes," said Demetrio, drawing the cream-coloured blanket round his shoulders, for it was a cold night and the moon which was advancing across his bed had a chilly look and he could not escape.

"Yes," he repeated, "I'll come."

"We'll have a marvellous trip if it doesn't rain."

"Provided it doesn't rain," he repeated a moment later, and as if to himself. Then he gave a sigh. His cheeks were flushed, and he had unbuttoned his pyjamas half-way down his chest, and his breathing was hard and irregular.

"Listen."

He spoke with eager confidence. He felt, he said, as if he was stripping himself naked. That was why he hesitated at first. And it was an embarrassing matter and words had never been his strong point and he had to go back so many years into the past.

He started talking. The shadow diminished as the moon set. It no longer pointed its muzzle nor gave a sudden jerk as before but up along the window-jamb, slender, its ears pricked up, it continued to shiver all the time Antonio was telling his story.

V

"This son of mine was born wise," his father had said, pointing at Antonio. "Some have soil where vines flourish and where maize and oats grow. But here we have tables and side-boards springing up. We will make a great cabinet-maker of him. I mean a crafts-man, perhaps even an original designer, if we give him a chance to study."

Antonio did study but without going to college to do so. He worked on his own, copying from life, going into a succession of offices, laboratories, workshops and sheds. He visited them all, and they became his garden into which as time went on, tables, side-boards, and chairs found their way.

Not bird-song but the hum of electric-saws and drills were music to Antonio. Instead of fig-trees or cherry-trees to shade him in the hot summer days he sought out scaffoldings and derricks. Smells of glue and tar replaced those of must and manure, and when he stretched himself out for a siesta, it was on platforms or piles of wood-shavings not on hay or corn-stubble.

He discovered how iron was worked, how bronze was smelted and witnessed the processes. He saw pot-tery baked, glass blown and rubber vulcanized. If walls were being built he would be there with his trowel; if they were soldering pipes, he was there to light the oxy-acetylene lamp. He helped to pump out the water when it had flooded the cellars.

He beat his ram rhythmically on the paving-stones of the piazza and he fixed tiles of various sorts on house-roofs.

In this way he watched things growing as they had grown in the far-distant parts of the country of which his father used to speak – seeds, earth, tools, patience. . . . Only, it was not the plough for him but the plane; not the spade but the rasp and the file. He did not prune, he sharpened tools with the grindstone. He did not hoe but bored holes with gimlets and drills.

He soon learned who were his enemies and how to fight them. They were not frost or drought, peronospora and phylloxera – they were woodworms, white ants, and wood-lice.

He could identify them in the workshop. He was in his element in a timber-shop where he was appointed as general watchman.

He would get up in the night and wander about among the rough timber and sawn planks, the panels and tables with his electric torch. He never seemed to feel sleepy. There among the bark, pith, and heart of the timber lurked the invisible thief boring holes in the wood, folding itself inside and gorging itself.

"It's the death-watch beetle," the owner had explained. A minute termite that made its call by beating its head against the gallery wall, drilling away. Antonio applied his ear to it. The red heart of the beech-tree, held captive, was shaking and the bare bodkin was piercing the smooth bark of the birch. Antonio listened. Extemporizing like a physician making an auscultation he diagnosed a cancer in the larch, a wasp in the pine, a stag-beetle in the chestnut, termites in the poplar. After the diagnosis he proceeded to the cure. He injected iron and zinc sulphates, smeared the trunks with tallow, paraffin, pitch; bathed them in hot and cold brine.

The death-watch beetle stopped its drilling, and panels and boards emerged from the workshop cured.

New arrivals came, in lorries. Trunks of spruce, white and Turkish acacia, baulks of birch, oak, pine, whole pear, and holly-trees.

Then the shop was filled with extraordinary smells, and though Antonio was half frozen, he took the precaution to keep a window permanently open. The chestnut gave off an odour of tanning which mingled with that of the cedar and pine; it nearly choked him. The pine went on weeping its resin for long enough and he wiped the tear-drops off the trunk.

When he had served a year, the owner promoted him to the laboratory. Antonio had put in a special request for this. Now that he was kept busy all day long he had less time for fishing out all the material he wanted from the river and had to give up visiting furnaces, foundries, offices, and big stores. On the other hand he was on the way to becoming a specialist.

And in point of fact he did. How impressed he was the day when to his ordinary tools were added compasses, bits, spirit-levels, grindstones, planes, and spoke-shaves. And when he planed the wood, with or against the grain, or turned and polished it, he was in his seventh heaven.

His early days as an apprentice seemed to have receded into the distance. The study he had put in at that time seemed crude and raw like the material he had been dealing with. No more watch duty now, no more sulphate injecting. Now he was concerned with animating the inertia of dead planks, formless baulks which were unloaded at daybreak at the doorways of the various departments.

He drew plans and made corrections; fashioned joints, bored, glued, veneered.

He made wheel-spokes, stakes, and ladders from acacia, matches and barrels from birch wood, lead-pencils from cedar. He coloured egriot-trees and cherry-trees and used them as mahogany for panelling, used dogwood for umbrella-handles, ash for billiard cues, willow osiers for baskets and chair-seats. He bent beech to required shapes and made sabots and hoops. He painted holly black and used it for ebony. He kept a watchful eye on walnut to see it was seasoning properly and did not warp. He prepared parquet flooring from service-tree wood and cut mirror frames from maple and pipes from its red roots.

He was equally at home with wood with straight, curved or marbled grains which he made into tobacco-jars. He became interested in musical instruments and experimented with the resonance of all the various woods. By dint of a number of tests he discovered the whole chromatic scale and supplied suitable woods for the instrument-maker – lime for keyboards, spruce for violin bellies, box for flutes and clarinets. He began to hear them "sing" and he found the sounds moving.

The trees came to him inert and wounded, their roots amputated. They left him fashioned ready for use, polished, veneered, lacquered and provided perhaps with three or four legs as the case might be, carved into oxen feet or lion-claws. They arrived in a confused pile and left in an orderly procession. Rough planks shaped into picture-frames, book-shelves, easy-chairs.

Dry and cracked tree-trunks, a hundred years old and more were turned or inlaid. Indian mahogany was grafted on to elm and native plane; the acanthus flower blossomed from the walnut wood and straw-berry and oak leaves were carved in beech wood. When the time came for them to go, they left the work shop and swayed gracefully on the porters' shoulders. Some went to a seaside town, some to far-off outposts, some were destined to pass through seaports and cross the sea and forest land. But for the most part they returned to their starting point.

Perhaps, thought Antonio, as he watched them go by, the fellow tree, with its root still deep in its native earth in some glade or forest, will be aware of his companion passing by.

And he became conscious of the deep silence to which nature had condemned them, and now, in contrast, the silence seemed terrible.

"Supposing we weren't here to extract music from them! . . ." And he would place his fingers on the keyboard of a grand piano, on the lime-wood and ebony keys, and the voice of the walnut and rosewood sounded, high-pitched or solemn, in the enclosed space of the workshop.

He would suddenly drop the lid.

"You need the tuner," remarked the instrument-maker.

It was true; now that he knew how to make the instruments he must learn to tune them; tune them in their proper setting and for a specific purpose.

He set to work to do so. Once more he found himself at the beginning again. He studied the progress and evolution of period styles, learned to differentiate between early Gothic and the later ogival, collected information about sedilia and tripod tables. He was amused at the vagaries of rococo, charmed by the flamboyant and learned to admire the picturesque element in the finished work.

He frequented dealers and antique shops. Sometimes he shivered with surprise mingled with apprehension. A strange, musty smell seemed to surge up from the past, from the Empire sideboards with their bronze-gilt handles, from the carved tables of all the Louis periods, from the lacquered Venetian sofas. Collected up from palazzi or any odd place, they lay piled up in the back of the shops, staid and wise. Specimens of an outmoded moded style, they had been washed up high and dry on to the banks by the tide of fashion and there they struggled, out of their element, like civil servants of a régime that has suddenly been overturned but whose intimate habits and secrets they are still able to reveal.

On one quest or another there were few places of interest which he did not visit. After he left the workshop he wandered everywhere. He became friendly with an old restorer who was kind and patient enough to explain to him from living and vibrating examples of furniture the appropriateness of each piece to its own place and time. From the same old man he learned how to appreciate the function of each piece, to recognize and discriminate between the part played by the craftsman and the artist, to judge between the gracefulness of caprice and the necessity for discretion. Thus he learned not to laugh at the huge canopied beds and the three-legged stools of his predecessors. They had functioned just as efficiently as the high modern bar stools and the motor-car upholstery mass-produced in the factories, just as well as modern lie-lows for the beach and the complicated hairdressers' chairs which, duly provided with the requisite guarantee, left the big stores every day.

When old Orazio had passed on his knowledge he bid him go. Now Antonio was really wise as his poor father had wanted him to be. Wise, but lonely.

He began to haunt the river again and fish out tables, broken cart-wheels, and posts. He made a skilful use of them with a coat of paint and lacquer. The two rooms and kitchen took on a new aspect, and Assunta began to sing as she rearranged the house, washed the dishes, sewed one pair of curtains and then another, embroidered a cloth which she spread on the marble table where their meals were taken. And she never stopped singing.

Antonio heard her.

She busied herself about the house, nimble and energetic. She put a shine on all the brasswork and polished every piece of glass. She also covered every box, chest of drawers and book-case with a kind of blue oil-cloth and the bulbs of each lamp with a parchment coloured paper. She knelt down on the floor and wax-polished every tile under the bed and cupboards. And she sang more cheerfully than ever and even whistled behind the curtain as she took a shower bath in the bath-tub that her brother had fixed up for her in a corner of the passage.

And Antonio heard her singing. He saw that she

was taking more trouble with her hair and had cut a fringe on her forehead and was trying to look after her small finger-nails, corroded by soda and lye, and her hands, that were swollen with chilblains.

"I say, have you fallen in love?"

He had caught her measuring a half-finished green woollen glove against her hand.

"No. What put that idea into your head?"

She blushed to the roots of her hair. The glove had slipped from her hand on to the floor like a heavy vine-leaf.

He retrieved it.

"Nothing. I was only joking. You've made yourself look so attractive."

VI

Then he had fled.

Four planks of wood, a few strokes of the plane, a pot of paint and he had almost revolutionized Assunta's life.

His heart raced warmly in his breast as he moved round, swift but silent. He too would have liked to sing some tuneless litany.

He ran off in the direction of the river, into the open.

"You've made yourself look so attractive," he repeated.

Four more planks of wood, then eight, twelve and finally twenty-four, springing, rushing into life violently, then subsiding calmly into a corner. Now they could quietly function for meals, sleeping and love-making. His was the joy of making them sing again.

And he laughed. He lay back and laughed. And meantime the river swept solemnly by at his feet with scarcely a ripple on the surface among the weeds.

God! If he could burst in among Carmine's broken-down wooden cupboards and get rid of them, he would hear his grandmother Filomena singing from the landing.

And he laughed.

"Have you gone mad, granny?"

And then he would rush down to Adriana's cellar and climb up the building opposite by each flight of stairs and bring them out in a long procession. Breaking through doors and suspicions, conquering habits, getting rid of all those tired springs, that jaded upholstery, those worm-riddled chests-of-drawers in which the death-watch beetle nightly had its fill.

What a mad course it would be! A relentless scramble wherever he appeared. No – even if he didn't appear his presence was not really necessary.

"O God," he murmured, dropping on his knees. "O God, even You did not appear. Yet You created things and have always done so. We do not know what Your tools were but You must have some. I've only got planes, saws, and hammers. O Lord help me!"

He spoke in an almost inaudible whisper; his knees

were pressed on the clay ground, his eyes fixed on the yellow road which swung gracefully past him.

"Help this your creation in whatever he tries to make! So that he may always persevere and never give up."

Having finished his prayer, he rose to his feet.

The water rippled and gurgled louder and louder in the silence as it lapped the reeds and earth bank; the white teeth of the gravel-bed smiled up at him.

He had come here to kneel down, here at the threshold of his mine; the mine that had served him so generously all these years. It flowed peacefully past now, relieved, cold and confident, with a calmness that helped to soothe the frenzied beating of his heart. He must go down to Adriana's and arrange about the removal of her old furniture at once.

"But why, Antonio?"

Her green eyes which always looked slightly wild, flashed in the darkness.

"Because you are going blind in here."

"It's a dark cavern of a place, and one feels suffocated in the confined space between these walls."

He would have a set-to at these walls with his pick and they would collapse into dust. Yes; he could see a white-maple wood partition replacing the three existing partition walls. All you would have to do would be to give it a push and it would roll up quietly like a spring-blind, beckon it back and you would have your wall again. The second wall likewise; it would slide discreetly to one side and there would be a drawing-room when occasion required. Adriana's customers could come and try on their dresses at leisure; they could come and see themselves in the mirrors he would fix in every corner of the room and even on the ceiling. Mirrors of every shape and size. The walls should be painted blue and sea-green to increase the sense of spaciousness and light. For light, pouring from the strip-lighting as the maple-wood screen slid back, would at last come triumphantly into its own.

He would enlarge the space, exploit it. Adriana would be able to continue with her dress-making but no longer in a prison.

He knocked at the door.

"Is it you, Antonio?"

He entered and sat down. "It's quite a step from the river to here."

He looked round him. Adriana had picked up her needle again and was sewing hard.

"I say, you're going blind in this hole!"

She did not reply. The needle slid deftly into the silk, making a faint scratching sound, as it passed through it. She sewed on and on. She brought the lamp near so that she could see to thread the needle.

"Good heavens, it's half-past eight."

The train could be heard whistling in the station. "I shall have to work all night. I have to deliver it to-morrow. And to think that I haven't stirred out all day! Has it been fine?"

He did not reply.

Whatever the weather; snow or hail, Adriana ought to have something to look at. He would contrive it somehow.

He snatched an inch-tape from its case and went up to the wall. It's low, he thought, but a window can be let in; concealed neon lighting would let a diffused light through. A couple of fixtures, a couple of glass panes, a pair of lace curtains and the whole thing becomes a reality. But only if Adriana would consent to have it opened up.

"We can't have this bare wall."

The folding partitions of maple-wood would divide the space in a new way, the mirrors multiply it, the windows would no longer merely reveal one scene and one scene and season only. You just pull a cord and a blind will occupy the space, a blind with a landscape painted on it.

"Adriana!"

She did not reply.

"We'll paint a seascape on it."

"A seascape?"

"Yes, in the window embrasure."

She bent over her sewing. She was counting stitches with the edges of her lips, and cutting notches with her scissors.

"A sea. More than one! Carmine tells me that the North Sea is brown and is drawn off behind the moon. Then it repents, returns and starts off again! And the ships with their sails lowered show their naked keels on the beach. And you should see it when the tide is flowing back with an edge of breaking foam and a procession of sea-gulls spearing at it, squawking and crying. Brown and wicked it is, but I would have it in the window, yellow like a field of ripe corn in a hot noonday sun, solid as my river is with a pair of ravens flying over it and a host of seagulls. A drunken moon-sea."

He became silent again. He had moved over to the table and was now following her progress with his eyes. She was making every effort to see that each flower matched the adjoining one.

"I can't make them meet. There isn't enough material," she said.

"And if other people consider this sea pale and hostile, you will only need to change windows, Adriana, and throw it open to them and they will find the sea that growls round our coasts, the vast, blue sea, fascinating and chaste with a volcano or two erupting in the background. . . .

"We will summon famous painters. By heaven, we've had enough darkness! We've suffocated long enough in here. I mean to conquer the seasons, contrive rainbows and forests here. We'll make love under the full moon . . . !"

Adriana had dropped her sewing, the scissors and the thimble as well.

"Antonio . . ."

He had taken her by the shoulders and was shaking her.

"The peaches here must ripen, not fade."

"Antonio . . ."

He had thrust her against the wall and was pressing against her. He was hot and covered with sweat, but pale.

"Did you really think I could leave you alone down here? . . ."

And he leaned back and laughed. A train interrupted them, screamed and went on. And the building vibrated. And Adriana remained motionless and quiet. Antonio laughed convulsively, rocking to and fro, violently and for no reason. He had slipped away from her towards the door and tried the handle several times but somehow he could not grip it properly and he roared and gasped with laughter.

Adriana, still riveted against the wall, followed these strange antics with her eyes, amazed at the outbursts of laughter so unlike the calm and silence which normally accompanied Antonio.

She watched him struggle to get out and finally lunge against the door which gave way and still laughing, Antonio hurled himself outside and his laughter erupted in the courtyard and spread all round like a peal of victory. At one time it was mingled with barking of a dog, at another with a yelp, then it vanished in the night, smothered by the moans of a goods train which, still stranded outside the station, was sending out long appeals for its usual siding.

VII

Now Demetrio was alone. Now he knew.

The moon had set. Having finished his story, Antonio had slipped into his own bed and fallen asleep. His quiet breathing rose and fell and the trains meanwhile continued to pass by and the clock to measure out its steps in the corner.

So that was why he had laughed on the staircase – he wanted to make love to Adriana in the moonlight out of season, among the ripe peaches! Within walls that slid away and turned on themselves silently like snakes to let them pass – and despite a volcano that erupted, a wave that broke and foamed behind every moon. So that was the cause of the laughter. And he had succeeded in breaking up and even multiplying the space down there. He had won the battle, he said. Again he heard that triumphant laugh – he too would burst into blossom, he thought!

"There is soil where the vine ripens."

There is irrigated land and arid land and arable land – where wheat and oats are sown, fertilized land that is naturally rich where the lemon and the olive grow and flourish. . . .

"But here large and small tables and side-boards spring up. Tell me, Niccolino, have you ever seen a man burst into blossom?"

Nicola laughed.

He closed the lift door and bit into his hunk of bread. He shook his head. No, he had never seen that, not even in a dream.

"Have you?"

"Yes."

He idly nibbled at his bread.

"Yes, I have seen one."

Nicola laughed again.

"I say, you must show me. I've seen thistles, potatoes, roses in plenty. But a man . . ."

He shook his head. He put the bread down on the step and wiped his brow.

"But I'd like to break out into blossom, myself!"

And he pressed his hands together and began to walk to and fro on the stair-carpet.

"Demetrio!"

He wanted to ask him what colours he would want his flowers to be but realized that Demetrio was worried.

"Sit down, Demetrio."

He picked up his crust and held it out to him.

"No, I'm not hungry."

He wasn't hungry. His face was pale and he sighed.

"Yes, really burst into flower. They would spring up from here, my knuckles. They would spring out after you'd fed them with patience and hard work. We shouldn't need a hoe or a rake but a plane, press, glue, oven, nails, varnish. We should have to hammer, saw, glue, and inlay. And they would invade the world on their own. Niccolino, look . . ."

T.S.—M*

He gripped hold of his arm.

"They've started already. Look."

He raised the dust-sheet and there they lay on the counters as usual.

"Look."

Nicola looked and chewed his bread. Demetrio pressed his wrist.

"Do you see?"

"Yes, I see."

A blue soup-bowl, a chest-of-drawers made in walnut, a folding bed, a miniature microscope, a bread-mixer with an enormous convex belly. A rubber flipper. A suite of furniture in rosewood.

"Do you see?"

"Yes."

He saw what he saw every day of his life.

Towels in piles. Rows of umbrellas.

"They've bent the beechwood round."

Nicola followed Demetrio. The latter pointed, shook, felt various objects. His walk became a trot, his trot a canter, his canter a gallop.

"They've injected sulphates. They've painted them with tar."

He tapped the cherrywood floor.

"No death-watch beetle here."

He tapped again.

"It won't warp again now."

He stepped on to the escalator.

"Come along."

He raised a curtain and felt. Steel is cold but rustless.

"Propelling pencils, paint-brushes."

He unwrapped the instructions for use and handed it to Nicola.

"Read it."

He unfolded another.

"Cast iron."

He handed it to him.

"Pure copper."

He pointed to the description on the label, murmured it and passed it over.

"Take this along. Take it home and study it. Antonio has read it heaps of times."

His voice quivered.

"Heaps of times," he repeated, "and now he's mastered it. After years of it. I can remember it all. Sometimes he went down to the river to fish. He came back and glued things. He began with a work bench and it was successful. He designed a table and he made that too. . . ."

He kept pointing things out and talking. He talked about the wood-work shop, the resin drops of the pinewood, the colouring of the egriot and cherry-trees and the red heart of the beech and the poplar parasite. He spoke quietly to himself rather than to Nicola and went on and on, finally getting back to the theme of blossoming forth into flower which was topmost in his mind just now.

"Going down."

"Going up."

Nicola watched him working the lift. They met on the landing and then each of them went his own path, each in his own shaft.

"Haberdasherypyjamasbracesmenswear . . ."

VIII

During the days that followed Demetrio talked and Nicola listened. Fascinated but incredulous he accompanied his friend as he wandered among the goods on show and pointed out first this and then that; each thing was individual, even when it was one of the mass-produced articles displayed on the counters.

"Look at the power they have. Humble but confident. They're in no hurry but all the same they're ready to leap into action."

Ink-stands, kettles, spring-blinds, suitcases, gloves, taps.

"The person who inspired them has vanished. So has whoever cut, stuck or spun them. Perhaps he's still making, cutting or spinning in some workshop. Or perhaps he's dead and all that's left of him now is this blossoming."

Curious blossoming, thought Nicola. Galalith, fibre, toughened aluminium!

"Here's the chance to act still and serve – for food, sleep, and love-making. He's breathed his own spirit into it, a little each day. Yes, he's animated them, that man who has now vanished, but he's present every day, without knowing it. . . ."

He was holding a coffee-pot in his hand and his hands were trembling.

What Antonio had wanted to do was to continue in work which would be carried on by others. Reproduce himself and hand himself on.

"It might be a dinner-service or a divan-bed or a white sliding partition. Escaping death in a hundred and one forms. Humble forms, it is true, but not to be underrated. What power! Nicola. You have seen for yourself what a steady demand there is for them here everyday."

The customers arrived avid for such things, asked for them, handled everything, trying shirts and shoes for size, applying various garments to their chests, head, and legs.

Demetrio put down the coffee-pot but his hands still continued to tremble.

"I can't explain it, Nicola, but it is impossible for me to go on working this lift. I must have my share, like Antonio; become part of the things I create, have my place on people's tables, invisible. I shall be there although no one will know. I must be there. I cannot wait. Just imagine, when you and you alone can say here one day that this article has a look of lift-boy number 2, Demetrio . . ."

He gripped Nicola by the shoulders.

"You will be department manager by then. You will have me put on show in the windows during the sales and I will pass by to see myself . . ."

"Yes, I'll offer you among the latest novelties!"

"With the loudspeaker."

"I will launch you with a new slogan."

"In the trade catalogue."

"In the market. I will seek you out in every piazza."

"I shall be out of stock by then."

"I'll order you by telegraph."

"And I will be produced again as a 'repeat'."

"You'll have to work day and night; you'll get no peace."

"I will honour every order."

"I'll export you."

"I'll let myself be exported."

"They'll make imitations."

"I will sue every imitator – with the full rigour of the law."

"But the Frog will find where you're hiding!"

"Who?"

"The Frog."

"Yes."

He blushed.

"I'll have to face him one fine day," he murmured.

"If you can pluck up courage."

"But I will."

And he gave a deep sigh.

"I'll ask for an interview tomorrow."

"When?"

"Tomorrow."

IX

"For three days I have been waiting, Sir. It has seemed a very long time"

The room had grown dark.

"For three days I've been kept in suspense."

He rose to his feet.

"Three days," muttered the Frog. "And I suppose they have seemed interminable to you?"

Demetrio nodded.

"But they're over now."

"Now?"

"Yes, you can go."

"Immediately?"

"Immediately, my boy."

"Thank you, Sir."

There was a rustle, a sound of shuffling feet. A door creaked.

"He's gone."

Up to a few minutes before, Demetrio had been pacing up and down like a caged bird, battering itself against the bars. Upset but sure of himself. He had threatened, invoked, laughed.

"He's gone."

The Frog heaved himself out of his leather armchair.

"We'll give him military honours!"

His ageing and weary face was lit momentarily by a wistful smile.

"The lift-boy has been hatching this out in silence without a word to anyone."

He switched out the light.

"Crazy idea!" he muttered and moved slowly towards the door, his legs splayed out, breathless with emotion.

He was conscious of the great store spread out there below him. It was empty of voices, dark and seductive. Flags and banners still marked out the field which he was daily accustomed to inspect and which now lay abandoned, deserted with the first breath of night air, for him alone to see. The escalator pulleys were silent too; the lifts, abandoned by their pilots, had gone down to dry-dock and were silent also.

There was a complete stillness in the grave and solemn atmosphere. The wash-hand basins leaned forward, resignedly offering their bosoms as the Frog slipped past them. He glided by mistrustfully. He advanced, shaken and unsure of himself. Still calm but breathing heavily with the floor-boards creaking dreadfully under his weight, interrupting the silence.

"They'll be warping next!"

He paused. The price-ticket had slid off a sewing machine and lay upside down. He leaned forward to read it and restored it to its right position. A diffuse light coming in from the street lamps outside found its way through the venetian blinds and caught the bright copper of the wires, the enamel on the refrigerators and the chromium-plate on the paste-mixers.

He let his glance sweep up and down among the goods. Although they were arranged in their usual positions on the floor, they seemed to be getting in his path. He threaded his way through this labyrinth in the gathering darkness from one department to the next in this climate of uneasy tranquillity, like an animal in hostile terrain. He hopped froglike between the billiard tables and other game-tables similarly covered with green baize and service-trolleys in shaped birchwood. He touched an article here and there, fingered it, caressed it. One was cool to his hand, another soft and velvety.

"This has been planed against the grain," he murmured.

And he stooped over it to study it. The grain of the table's surface seemed to run along monotonously, with the occasional knot, the ecstatic centre of a whirl-pool, a meeting-place of currents which had arranged themselves in attractive arabesque patterns.

He had put on his spectacles and was examining the surface of the white, unstained oak, the beech ply-wood, the metal-tubing, the rubber cushioning. Soft as flesh or unbelievably cold, the various objects slid by him silently.

The Frog stooped down and felt the various

objects. Inert, they all submitted. Full of amazement he handled them, lifted the dust-sheets, unfolded the directions-for-use, and in the twilight calculated figures, made out names, deciphered voltages and specifications.

"Iron legs."

"Television parts."

He groped his way in the dark and fumbled about among the television sets, unwrapped parts, extracted plugs and terminals.

"It's fantastic," he murmured.

It was the first time he had ever found himself rummaging about in the mysteries of the insides. Entrails of various sorts gradually yielded themselves up to him, and slowly he aligned them, putting certain items on one side, connexions and rings, welded or paired together, round, oblong, hooked. Some made of rustless steel, others of plastic; and there were nails and screws and washers. They lay scattered on the counter like characters of some unfamiliar alphabet or pieces of a jig-saw puzzle of the kind children put together with such skill and patience. . . . If only Demetrio were there. . . .

"Demetrio?"

He swung round. It was a refrigerator.

"Demetrio!"

He moved away from the counter, walked round the refrigerator. The flour-mixer below him gave a slow yawn.

"Demetrio!"

He moaned several times as he staggered forward with out-stretched arms, his round eyes opened fantastically wide. He fixed his gaze on a corner and steered towards it. It turned out to be a stove, a porcelain stove standing on the floor, its narrow flue rising up in the semi-darkness. He leaned against it heavily. It was cold and he pressed his chest desperately against its edges. A terrible fit of exhaustion suddenly overcame him, and he gripped the porcelain neck of the stove with both hands.

"He has done for me," he murmured.

His glance wandered vaguely among the motionless shadows in the store.

"He has done for me," he said. "And how he's enjoyed doing it!"

He tightened his grip on the neck of the stove which it continued to extend indifferently towards him.

"Shirkers!"

A wave of anger went through him, he gave a jerk of his back and stood erect.

So it was here they were coming to hide themselves away, under his very nose and yet outside his control; yes, here among the goods which he had been looking after for more than thirty years.

"Maybe in a dinner-service, a divan-bed or a white sliding partition . . ."

Those had been the words he had overheard in the conversation between Demetrio and the lift-boy at number 2. And the latter was prepared to aid and abet him; had promised to launch him, export him.

A sinister laugh disturbed the peace of the floor. He moved on, laughing, making his way among the wares which he thrust angrily aside.

"Get out . . . get out . . .!"

They slipped between his legs or slid by on a level with his face. With cold, lascivious leers the tailor's dummies tempted him with an "exceptional offer" in blue double-breasted suitings.

"Get away!"

They barred his path. He extracted his notebook from his pocket, put on his spectacles, stood by the window and wrote something down. He underlined the words "thin it out".

"Thin it out," he hissed.

The little boy would get out of this tangle all right; he would dash away contentedly far from the cage that went up and down. He could see him against a pillar, confidently handling his drill, flushed as when he had been describing it. And the electric saw was humming away.

He could see him anxious yet fierce, emerging from a area of marquetry, sinking into a hoop, gliding into a small mirror.

He stretched out a hand.

"Wait for me!"

Had he got him?

"Don't run away!"

He clenched his fist and hit out.

There was a thud and a splintering of glass. He had struck too hard. He opened his hand; the inlaid wood frame was intact, the vine-leaf pattern was broken in several places, the glass was shivered.

"Demetrio . . ."

He raised the splinters of glass to his lips and kissed them with great tenderness and smiled. He caressed the inlaid vine-pattern, and with a deep sigh continued on his journey among the quiet shadows of the great shop, dazed, murmuring the name "Demetrio".